Melanie ~
what a genuine ~
friend you are ~
with Santa! Barba

# Christmas Dreams
# and Santa Schemes

by

## Barbara Lohr

Purple Egret Press

Purple Egret Press
Savannah, Georgia 31411

Cover Art: The Killion Group
Editing: Bev Katz Rosenbaum

## Dedication

For every family.

May all find peace and love.

# Chapter 1

The smell of fresh bread welcomed them when Sarah ushered Nathan and Justin into the back room of The Full Cup. Her cheeks and lips felt chapped, and she closed the door on the cold December day. "We finally made it." She got busy unwinding the scarves that covered her little boys' faces.

"I hate winter." Yanking off his mittens, Nathan threw them on the floor.

"Nathan," Sarah said, raising her voice over the rock music. She'd tackle that in a minute. "Please put those on the sink to dry." With the heat in this room, it wouldn't take long. Grumbling, her five year-old did as he was told while she tended to Justin.

Her three year-old stared up at her, eyes solemn and blonde hair upended when she whisked off his cap. "Thank you, Mommy." He was way too serious for a boy his age.

She tousled his hair. "You're welcome, handsome boy. Hang your jacket up, please. You too, Nathan." Her voice rose. Her hands stayed on her hips until Nathan did as he was told.

Christmas was bearing down on them. The fragrance of pumpkin pies had barely faded from The Full Cup when Christmas ads began to blare from the TV, glittering with holiday cheer.

Not for her. Not this Christmas.

But what about her boys? The war in a country far across the ocean meant nothing to them. But it had taken their daddy. Jamie would want Nathan and Justin to have a good Christmas. Whatever it took, they would get what they wanted. Sarah hitched up the jeans that wouldn't button any more.

Emotional eating. She was all about it.

Now, the music. Ryan's loud music throbbed in her ears, not exactly the fluffy stuff that would raise your sprits. Jamie's younger brother would be deaf by the time he was thirty. "Turn the radio down!" she called out, slipping off her coat and hanging it on one of the hooks. Her day of babysitting for seven small children had gone well but left her exhausted. She'd formed the group with her friend Lindsay and other young mothers in Gull Harbor.

The oven clanged shut behind her. "The music, Ryan. Please."

"Okay, boss lady."

The teasing smile in Ryan's voice wore on her like summer sand in her sandals. Sarah hated his nickname for her—a sure sign of his immaturity. She helped the boys off with their boots and snowpants. The music changed to a Christmas favorite about having "holly jolly" Christmas. Good luck with that but at least the volume had dropped. "Thank you, Ryan. Nathan and Justin, set your boots on the rug next to the door."

The warmth of the room seeped into her bones. Usually her mother worked back here but the heavy trays had become too much. Mom had suggested that Ryan might help out if he had time. But they couldn't afford to pay her brother-in-law, so it felt like begging. "All the cookies you can eat," she'd joked when she brought it up.

"No problem," Ryan had said, shifting his stance the way he did when his old injury bothered him. "Do you mind if I split the shift? Cookies in the morning and bread dough at night?"

"Of course not." After all, he worked full time at Branson's Motors. "I appreciate your help."

He'd given her a lopsided grin. "This will be my Christmas present. Not the Porsche I had my eye on for you."

Always kidding. "A Porsche," she'd sputtered.

So far, Ryan had been reliable. Every morning he was here when she arrived and he closed up at night, driving up Red Arrow highway in between shifts to work at the garage. Jamie would be proud of him.

She'd just have to live with this for a few weeks. If it weren't for the Christmas baking, she could handle the back work room alone. But her taxes were way overdue. She needed to keep the display cases full and the cash register ringing.

Staring at herself in the mirror above the coat hooks, Sarah wondered who this woman was. Her hair was a rats' nest and dark circles smudged her eyes. Who had time for makeup? Fluffing her tangled curls, she caught sight of the image reflected in the mirror. "Oh, my."

Muscles flexed under the gray T-shirt of the man hoisting trays from the oven. A mop of curly hair hid his face. Just for a moment her heart stopped. *Jamie.* How many times had she seen her husband like this, shuffling the trays like cards in his poker game with the guys? Her throat closed and a tear squeezed from her eye.

The man turned. Ryan.

Of course. Only Ryan.

"What is it?" He swept the damp hair from his forehead.

"Nothing." She hoped he didn't notice her damp eyes.

"I didn't expect you back today. Usually you go straight home after picking up the boys."

Running her hands over her jeans and a tattered *Say Yes to Michigan!* sweatshirt, Sarah felt frumpy. "My mother wasn't answering her phone."

He nodded toward the stairway. "She went up to her apartment a while ago. You should have called me instead of driving over. The streets are slippery."

"I—I managed. Think I'll just run up and check."

Grabbing a sheet of caraway rye from the oven, Ryan shoved it onto the cooling rack. Then he shut the oven with a clang and ripped off the protective mitts with his teeth. "I locked the front door. No one came in after three. The snow, you know."

"Did my mother look sick?"

"Maybe a little flushed. Lila's getting older, Sarah." He propped a hip against the work counter.

"I know." As if she needed reminding. Giggling and jostling, the boys disappeared into the front of the coffee shop.

"No cookies!" Sarah called out. "You haven't had dinner yet."

Silence out front. Ryan chuckled and they exchanged a glance. "Double trouble," she said.

"They're good boys, Sarah. And I've got news." His lips twisted into a smile. "Boys are trouble."

*Well, he should know.*

"Just one cookie?" Nathan's wheedling voice called from the front.

"It can't hurt." Ryan always took their side. "One cookie, Mom?"

"You're no help at all." Sarah got tired of saying no. That was her role now. Disciplinarian. Not a wife, just a mother. "Okay. Just one. Then you both get back here." After a suspiciously long time, they burst through the swinging door, waving oatmeal cookies.

Going over to the butcher block table in the center of the room, Nathan ran a hand over the floury surface and munched. "Aren't you cold in just your undershirt, Uncle Ryan?"

Embarrassment flooded Sarah's face. "Nathan, don't be rude."

But the comment didn't seem to bother Ryan. "I wear this because it's hot in here. And I think you owe me a bite from your cookie." But just as Ryan reached to snatch it, Nathan offered the cookie up. He gave his uncle a sweet smile that tugged at Sarah's heart. Ryan was right. They were good boys. Taking a tiny bite, Ryan chewed with exaggerated lip movements.

"Nice. Real nice," she said. He could be such a clown with the kids.

One hand smushed across his face, Justin giggled, peaking at his uncle from between his fingers.

"Are you laughing at me? I'll sic the tickle bug on you." Ryan made a move to scoop Justin up, but he ran around the end of the table. They adored Uncle Ryan. Sarah just didn't want them turning out like him.

"You boys are getting cookie crumbs all over my workroom," Ryan said.

"Now you sound like me." Sarah chuckled. But Ryan's comment brought the boys up short. Walking to the wastebasket, they dusted the crumbs off their hands.

"Man, it's hot in here." Ambling over, he shoved open a window. Muscles rippled as he moved, his limp hardly noticeable. She'd never noticed those etched biceps.

"You are hot," she murmured. *Oh mercy.* "*Warm.* I mean warm. It's so warm in here." Sarah fanned herself. What was she saying?

"Yes. It is," he said, turning slowly, the hint of a smile dancing across his lips.

Sarah clapped her hands. "Okay, time to check on Grandma." She herded the boys toward the back stairs. "We'll be right back. Have to check on my muscles. I mean, my mother."

"I'll be here." Ryan adjusted his apron. "Still have lots of work to do."

"Right. You just...get to work." Why was she so rattled?

"You bet, boss lady."

"I wish you wouldn't call me that." My, her nerves really were on edge.

"Sorry. I'm just teasing." He didn't look sorry at all.

Her heart was racing. Must be the heat. "I'll be right back."

Escaping to the stairs, Sarah led the boys up to the second-floor apartment over the shop. Her parents had lived up here from the very beginning. Sarah remembered her dad getting up in the dark to go down and set the bread dough to rise. Jamie had taken on the role after her dad passed away. Their own house wasn't far away.

Sarah knocked on the door before cracking it open. "Mom? It's me. Sarah and the boys."

The TV was off. The living room, silent. The latest issues of *The National Enquirer* were neatly arranged on the coffee table. Her mother liked to stay current on her Hollywood news. Sarah sniffed. Usually Mom would be eating an early dinner. But no stew or a pork chop aroma hung in the air. She poked her head into the small kitchen. Nothing.

Sarah had planned to have grab bars installed in the bathroom. Her mother's Christmas present would be a safety system with a button to wear. One touch and EMS would come screeching to her aid.

Cold fear skittered down her spine. "Boys, sit on the sofa. Not a peep out of you." Eyes wide, they sat down.

"Mom?" As she walked down the long hall toward the bedrooms, a sweet smell drifted from the bathroom. Soap or perfume? Her mother was singing.

"Mom, are you in there?" She knocked on the door.

The singing stopped. Slowly the door cracked open. "Did you need me, sweetheart?"

Sarah stared. Green goop covered her mother's face.

The door closed. "Just give me a second. I'll be right out," her mother said above the sound of splashing water.

A face mask? Her mother had never shown interest in that kind of thing. Maybelline lipstick once a week and that was for church.

Walking briskly back to the living room, Sarah clicked on the TV and found *Sesame Street.*

"That's for kids," Nathan said with contempt, reaching for the remote.

"But I like the Count!" Justin whined. "Leave it, Mom. Please?"

Was there ever an end to this? "The two of you sit there and watch Big Bird. Period." She meant business and they heard it. Slumping onto the sofa, Sarah enjoyed the silliness of the show. Laughing together with her boys felt good. After fifteen minutes or so, her mother appeared.

"What a surprise." Mom's salt-and-pepper hair was pulled back with a pink headband Sarah had never seen before.

"Don't you look nice." Jumping up, Sarah came closer. Was her mother wearing eye liner and mascara? And that wasn't all. "Is that a new top, Mom?"

"Why, yes. Do you like it?" Mom fingered the white beaded snowflakes decorating the red knit sweater. "I got it at the Michigan City outlet."

"Have you lost weight?" Sarah couldn't help the faint note of jealousy in her voice.

"Maybe just a tad." Mom patted her hips in the snug beige pants. "How did the babysitting go today?"

"We call it playschool. Fine. Not that I'd want to do it every day." That was an understatement. She'd lose her mind, wiping noses and helping with puzzles for all those children.

Sarah's mother had not been in favor of the co-op. She'd been Sarah's main babysitter since the boys were born. But she was getting older. Now was time for her mother to relax—watch soap operas or read romance novels. "What was that stuff on your face?"

"An avocado mask." Mom ran a veined hand over her cheeks. "Supposed to help the wrinkles. Mine are terrible. What do you think?"

Sarah leaned closer. "You've always had beautiful skin."

"Has Ryan started on the Christmas cookies?" her mother asked in an obvious attempt to change the subject.

"Maybe tomorrow." Her mother had baked the Christmas cookies as long as Sarah could remember. The buttery rich thimbles, layered mint chocolate brownies, tangy lemon bars, spritz and the sand tarts – those were all her mother's making. The cookies took time and delicate shaping. Ryan had large capable hands, suitable for punching down bread dough and wrestling with Harleys. "I hope this works out."

Pink lips pursed, Mom sank into the barcalounger that had been her father's favorite chair. "Ryan will be a big help. You can teach him."

"Right." Sarah hated to admit that she missed talking to the customers. Baking cookies with Ryan in the back room? That kitchen could feel mighty small. She plopped down on the sofa.

"Mom! You're squishing me." With a gentle shove, Justin moved over. Both boys were listening to this conversation with great interest.

"I guess so. Gull Harbor folks do love their Christmas cookies." Today the holiday expectations of her home town made her weary.

"They do indeed." Her mother nodded so hard, Sarah thought the pink headband might fall right off. "Soon all storefronts will be decorated with lights. The painted reindeer will sprint over Whittaker Street. We add to the Christmas cheer with our cookies."

Eyes bright, Lila glanced at her daughter for agreement.

Well, at least someone had the Christmas spirit.

"But what does Ryan know about Christmas cookies?"

Lila's eyes sparkled. "What he doesn't know you can teach him. You taught Jamie. How about some hot dogs, boys?"

"Hot dogs!" When Nathan and Justin bounced on the sofa, it made Sarah's head hurt. You'd think they never got hot dogs at home. Everything always tasted better at Grandma's.

The day was feeling longer by the minute. Sarah pushed herself up, trying to hide her stomach roll by tugging down her sweater. "Sounds like you've got things covered. I'll go down and talk to Ryan about the cookies."

When Sarah reached for the door knob, she noticed a pile of books on a side table. "What's this, Mom?" She picked one up. *"The History of the Roman Empire."*

Her mother twirled a gray curl around one finger. "Just thought I'd read up on things."

"Right." *The Roman Empire?*

Making her way downstairs again, Sarah reached for the handrail. She felt as if she'd been transported to someone else's life. Back in the work room, Ryan was standing in front of the big refrigerator. One muscled arm held the door open.

"What are you doing?" That open door was giving her a chill

Ryan turned. "Figuring out the butter. Your mother said you would take me through the recipes."

She expelled a breath. "Okay. Let's start there." Going over to her desk, she took the big blue binder from a shelf. Someday she had to organize this collection of slip sheets and clippings. Flipping through, she found the thimbles recipe. Ryan hovered nearby, smelling like a man who'd worked hard. Sarah had always liked that familiar scent. But Ryan hadn't been the man.

"Thimbles?" Ryan read over her shoulder.

"Didn't your mother make them?" The jam-filled thimbles were one of her favorites.

"My mother always said that if God had wanted women to bake he wouldn't have invented bakeries."

"How awful!" The words were out before she could think. Ryan and Jamie's parents had moved back to Chicago about the time that Jamie and Sarah were married. Shortly after that, they'd divorced. Mrs. Pickard had remarried and their father had died in a traffic accident. Neither Jamie nor Ryan had taken to their mother's new husband.

Bringing her attention back to the recipe, Sarah tried to focus. "Or we could do the mint-layered brownies."

He looked offended. "Trust me. I can handle the thistles."

"Thimbles. Okay then. Thimbles it is." She drew herself up. "Let's leave three pounds of butter out to soften tonight."

Sarah watched him walk to the refrigerator. Ryan was a good-looking man and she couldn't understand why he wasn't dating someone. His limp was hardly noticeable.

Shortly after that, Sarah collected the boys and got them dressed for the weather. Then they left for home.

As usual, that night she told Jamie all about her day, his picture on her lap as she lay in bed. "Ryan's pitching in, Jamie." She finished up by reporting on his brother. "We'll see how that goes. He is good with the boys." Then she kissed the framed photo and set it back on her nightstand.

Settling under the covers, she tried to shake her misgivings. This Christmas felt all wrong. Somehow she would make it right.

~.~

"Christmas cookies." Ryan was fuming when he got to Branson Motors that night. Evening came early in December. The sky was dark as he pulled into the back lot.

They'd probably get more snow tonight. The wind nipped his cheeks and rattled the bare branches overhead as he locked the truck. When he got inside, Ryder Branson and his father Stanley were jawing about something in the back. Their chuckles echoed through the open office door as Ryan headed back. He'd never seen a father and son that close. Sometimes it got to him.

When he walked in, both men looked up.

"Here comes our new tenant," Stanley greeted him with his usual peppery tone.

Boots up on the desk, Ryder stretched back and grinned. "So how are you enjoying the apartment upstairs?"

"Suits me just fine." Ryan took an empty chair and unbuttoned his jacket. This wasn't the neatest office in the world but it served its purpose. Like a lot of the businesses along Red Arrow, the garage had been a fixture for years. The Bransons mostly worked on Harleys, which had been the main attraction of the job. "Thanks for renting it to me."

"Glad someone can use it," Ryder said. "Maybe the place will bring you good karma or whatever it is that Phoebe says."

Stanley wore a big grin. "Got me my favorite daughter-in-law back. Ryder couldn't wait to get out of here and back to his house in the woods."

"It was the woman in the woods that counted, Dad, not the house." Ryder and his wife Phoebe had been divorced for a year. During that time, Ryder had been one mean son of a gun, and his father hadn't been much better. How Ryder won Phoebe back, Ryan would never know. But it had something to do with fixing up their old house.

While they were divorced, Ryder had lived in the apartment over Branson Motors. With a bedroom and a kitchen, that apartment served its purpose, but it was nothing Ryan would want on a full-time basis. The smell of oil and grease crept up through the walls. It was a place, not a home.

Now Ryder sniffed the air. "Man, you smell good."

"Yeah, you're making me hungry." Stanley patted his stomach.

"It's the bread." Smiling, he slipped out of his heavy jacket.

"How's it going with the widow?" Ryder asked with an expectant grin.

"You make it sound like she's eighty." Before, she'd been his sister-in-law—the person who kept his brother happy with her sweet smile and soft curves. Now she talked to Ryan like a drill sergeant. So serious, her eyes dark with worry. He didn't know how to take her. The chair creaked when he shifted.

"Sarah's a pretty little thing and a good mother." Then Ryder stopped.

"She's had bad luck." Stanley snapped up a toothpick. He always had one handy. "Your brother was a patriot. I served in Vietnam, and I can't say enough good things about Jamie or Sarah. But it's a darn shame."

The mood had turned somber. Ryder nodded. "And that's the truth. So are you handling the two jobs okay? Not making you crazy or anything?"

"It's not a picnic chasing up and down Red Arrow in the snow," Ryan admitted.

"How does your schedule go?" Kicking back in his chair, Stanley studied him, that toothpick between his teeth. "You start the day there, come back to the garage for a few hours and then it's back to the bakery?"

"I'm burning a lot of gas, but I make sure I put in at least eight hours up here." Working on a Harley was bittersweet for him. But he knew those machines like the back of his hand. "You know anything about making thimbles?"

The foreheads of both men creased. "You mean like in sewing, son?" Stanley said. "My wife used a thimble on her finger sometimes."

"No. These are cookies." He almost hated to say the word.

"Cookies?" A grin lifted the corner of Ryder's mouth. "You're baking cookies with Sarah? I thought you were handling the bread."

Stanley put both hands on his stomach "Now you're really making me hungry."

Okay. This whole baking thing didn't sound very manly. But he was helping out. Sarah and her mother Lila needed him. "Yes, her mother added the cookies," he muttered. "I'm fine with it."

That brought a howl from both of them. "The widow's got you making dainty little Christmas cookies? With those ham-sized hands that have touched carburetors?" Stanley made some mincing movements with his fingers. Of course Ryder roared at his dad's antics.

"Glad you two are enjoying yourselves." Ryan's face burned.

"Why don't you bring back some samples?" Stanley ran one hand over his perpetual stubble. He only shaved every three days. "We can give your cookie skills a road test."

"I haven't made them yet."

Ryder gave him a curious look. "Anything going on with you and Sarah?"

Reaching down, Ryan played with his boot. By the end of the day, his shorter leg ached. "Of course not."

"Why not?" Ryder snorted. "She's a sweet woman with two cute little boys who need a dad."

"The emphasis is on sweet." Ryan looked up and frowned. "Not exactly my type."

"What does that mean?" Mouth hanging open, Stanley looked from his son back to Ryan.

"Dad, I think that means that our boy Ryan still likes women with swinging hips and lying lips." Ryder stabbed a finger at Ryan. "That's what got me into trouble at the Rusty Nail. And I wound up sleeping upstairs in that cold apartment. So watch it."

Ryan had never been known for good decisions. "What would Sarah want with me anyway?" He kicked out his bum leg.

Stanley kept working that toothpick. "You might be ugly as sin and cantankerous on certain days, but you look like marrying material to me."

Drawing his leg back, Ryan shook his head. "No way."

Ryder was frowning. "Your accident on the Harley was what, five years ago?"

"Four. And in case you haven't noticed, I'm not exactly a chick magnet. I wasn't even fit for service." It bugged him that he hadn't been able to go off and serve with Jamie.

But then, who would watch out for Sarah?

The only sound in the room was the ticking of the giant clock on the wall.

"Let it go, Ryan," Stanley said with disgust. "That was an addle-brained stunt, racing Zack Deiter down the highway. You could have got yourself killed. But put all that behind you. There's a lot more to being a man than walking straight."

"Easy for you to say." Getting up, Ryan stretched. Hours of bending over the work table or motorcycle engines made him stiff. "Time for some shut eye."

"Don't forget to come back with those cookies," Stanley called out as Ryan made his way through the garage.

"Right." Dragging himself up the stairs, Ryan felt

uncomfortable about that conversation. He didn't like discussing Sarah like that. When Jamie and Sarah were dating in high school, his mother had commented that Sarah was "too good to be true." Maybe she was right. Oh, she could talk tough with the boys but she was a cream puff underneath.

Ryan had made a promise to his brother, and he would watch out for Sarah. Even if it meant making cookies.

.

## Chapter 2

Her wise-cracking brother-in-law making cookies. Imagine that. Having dropped the boys off the next morning, Sarah hunched over the steering wheel. Traffic was light and overnight the roads had been plowed. She needed coffee bad. The heat in her old Pontiac couldn't keep up with Michigan's cold weather. Still shivering when she reached The Full Cup, she smiled to see Ryan's black pickup with flames painted behind the wheels. The boy would always be trouble.

Man, not boy.

She parked and went inside. The warmth of the workroom and the smell of bread comforted her. "Sure smells wonderful in here," she called out. The shuffling of metal baking sheets brought back memories of her dad and Jamie. Now Ryan was the man in front of the ovens and he turned.

"Morning." When Ryan heaved a tray of bread onto the cooling rack, she couldn't help but notice the strong shoulders and rippling biceps. Yep, definitely a man. As if she needed to be reminded.

Coffee always restored her sanity. She needed coffee.

"Still cold out there?" Ryan threw her one of his crooked

smiles.

"Freezing. And we're probably in for more snow." Tugging off her scarf, she unbuttoned her coat. "You can smell it."

"I don't think I've ever smelled snow, Sarah," Ryan said quietly, mischief swirling in his coffee-colored eyes. He had an intense, brooding quality about him, like a slow dark roast.

Now she really was losing it.

Sarah laughed. "Then you've missed it. Trust me, you can tell." She hung her red scarf on the hook. When she slid out of her coat, Ryan reached to help her. He smelled like warm bread and sweat. She liked the combination.

Smiling down at her, he said, "Your cheeks are all pink."

"It's freezing out there." She pressed both palms to her face. Her skin felt cold and dry. Maybe she needed one of her mother's avocado masks. "But it was probably much colder when you came in at five."

"About fifteen degrees." He hung up her coat.

"Why, thank you, Ryan." His thoughtfulness surprised her.

"I'll take cold weather over heat any day."

He was so close and she stared up into his eyes. "Your eyes are like coffee," she murmured.

"What?" Ryan jerked back.

Where had her silliness come from? "I said I could sure use some coffee."

*Stop the nonsense, Sarah.*

Enough. She trotted out to the storefront, flipping on lights as she went. In three minutes she had her warm mug of coffee. Sarah killed it with cream so it didn't look at all like Ryan's deep, brown eyes. Sighing, she slugged down a gulp and felt it wind through her in a warm stream. Her riotous imagination must be the result of holiday stress. Then it was back to the work room, her attitude adjusted and ready to work.

For an hour or so she turned out brownies, cheese crowns and pecan rolls while Ryan punched, shaped and baked bread. His rye rolls, a new addition, had been a big hit so he was making more of those. Every night, Ryan closed out the register. They'd been taking in more money since he'd started helping out and she hoped it continued.

While the pastries cooled, she checked the hunks of butter they'd left out the night before. "Feels like it's ready." She looked up to find Ryan studying her hands cupped over the wrapped packages. "What?"

He shrugged. "Nothing. It's just the way you hold the butter. You'd think those were your kids or something."

Sarah gave the butter a final pat and turned to the supply cupboard. "In some ways, they are, I guess. Want to chop the nuts?" She took down a bag of pecans.

Grabbing a knife from the rack over the sink, he said, "I'm on it."

"Good, you chop and I'll sift the flour." Reaching into the cupboard, she brought out the huge recipe binder. "Dad had everything in his head. Now it's all in this fat notebook, secret spices included."

"Sounds more like a spy mission than a recipe file." Spreading out the pecans, he started to chop, working the knife with studied determination.

She glanced around. "My dad took this business very seriously."

"I'm sure he did. The Full Cup is still here. That's saying something. Michiana Thyme is closed." The knife seemed to emphasize each point. That was a sore spot in the town. The dress shop Michiana Thyme had been an anchor in Gull Harbor for as long as Sarah could remember. But Loretta, the owner, had moved closer to her daughter. The store had never sold, so it closed. Now the green frame structure housed the town's PR department and even that was temporary.

No way did Sarah want to tank another Gull Harbor family business. Not on her watch.

"Yep, we're still here." But she couldn't think about the taxes due at the end of January. Usually, they paid twice a year but she'd skipped a payment. Revenues were down and she'd had unexpected expenses, like Jamie's funeral.

But she wouldn't think about that.

The ginormous binder was filled with clippings and scrawled ingredients, some in plastic slip sheets but most just crammed into the pages. A few fell to the floor. Dropping the knife, Ryan scooped them up. "Here let me take that."

"Thanks. The darn thing weighs a ton." She shifted the book into his arms. The brush of his skin sent a surprising burst of warmth up both arms. "Oh, my."

Ryan cocked a brow. "Oh, my what?"

She wet her lips. "Oh, my. Someday I've got to organize this."

Setting the binder on the table, he flipped it open. "You got a lot stuffed in here, that's for sure."

"We were afraid the recipes would be lost someday," she said, turning the pages. Then she pushed back the curly hair that would never behave. "But the way things worked out, what does it matter? There's no little girl to carry on with The Full Cup."

"Why does it have to be a girl?" Ryan studied her. She must look a mess, no makeup or anything. "Your dad handled the shop, right?"

"Yep. He mostly worked the coffee machine and my mother baked." She tried to picture Justin or Nathan running The Full Cup, but that was a stretch. "Jamie seemed to like the business."

"Jamie enjoyed *you*," Ryan said quietly, going back to his chopping. "He would have become a brick layer if you were standing next to him."

"Oh, Ryan. That's so sweet." His words sent a rush of comfort through her.

There was a time when Ryan always had a chip on his shoulder. Maybe the accident had changed him. But she didn't want to spend a lot of time analyzing her brother-in-law.

Time to get to work. "We need a little Christmas music." Walking to the old plastic radio on the shelf, Sarah snapped it on and turned to the station that ran only Christmas music, starting the week before Thanksgiving. "Have Yourself a Merry Little Christmas" was playing and she hummed along. She sure hoped her troubles would be out of sight in the coming year. While Ryan chopped the heck out of those pecans, she measured the flour.

Working side by side, she felt a bit of Christmas bloom inside.

His knife flying, Ryan said, "Besides, Sarah, there might still be a little girl in your future."

The flour sack slipped from her hands onto the counter. A puff of flour made her cough. "Don't be ridiculous, Ryan." She tried to catch her breath.

His head snapped back. Ryan had always been super sensitive. That had *not* changed.

"Sorry. I shouldn't have said that."

"Don't worry about it." Face closed and smile definitely gone, he kept chopping. "You're a good mother. You'll probably have other kids."

What was he saying? "How?"

Ryan's laugh came out dry as the flour still tickling her throat. "Do I have to spell out how to make a baby?"

Lordy, it was hot in here. Light footsteps sounded on the stairs. Her mother danced into the workroom, wearing black ankle boots with black pants and her green Christmas sweater. "Good morning," she sang out. Then she stopped. "Sorry. Am I interrupting?"

"Of course not." Grateful for the interruption, Sarah measured out the sugar. "We're starting on the thimbles."

"Now, don't you make a wonderful team?" Looking pleased, Mom unhooked her apron from the wall, tied it around her slender waist and disappeared through the swinging door.

Dumping her butter into the large mixing bowl, Sarah flipped on the beaters. They hit the bowl with an erratic, metallic rhythm.

"Everyone's gone crazy this Christmas."

Shrugging his unlawfully broad shoulders, Ryan murmured, "Sarah, Sarah."

"What? They have. Totally crazy." But she wasn't about to share her concern about her mother. The butter had become a smooth soft texture and she cracked two eggs into the bowl. The ding of the oven timer came as a relief. He stepped over to take out the sour dough bread that Finn Wheeler had ordered for the Mangy Mutt.

Concentrate. She had to concentrate. When the eggs and butter were thick and creamy, she slowly added the sugar. "Silver Bells" came on the radio and she hummed along. Behind her, Ryan opened and closed oven doors. The smell of bread expanded in the overheated room until she could almost bite into it. Wiping her forehead with the back of one hand, she stepped over to open a window.

"Thanks," Ryan said, starting on the pecans again. "But I can take the heat if you can."

Why did he continue to tease her? Sarah gave a frustrated sigh. "Let's just get to work."

"Yes, ma'am."

Okay, that *ma'am* made her feel as old as Mount Baldy, a mountainous dune that had been stretched along the Michigan shoreline forever. She'd concentrate on the cookies and not his comments. The sugar had blended in nicely so she slowly added the flour. A sidelong glance told her the pecans looked more like brown sugar than nuts. But she didn't say anything. No way would she hurt Ryan's feelings.

Out in the storefront, the bell jingled—music to her ears. The soothing sound of her mother talking to customers restored Sarah's sanity. After she added the vanilla and a touch of salt, the dough was ready. Now came the work. The point that would separate the bakers from the bad boys.

"It's time to separate the eggs, Ryan."

He looked at her. "What's that?"

"We roll the dough in the beaten egg whites so the nuts you chopped will stick to the cookies."

"O—kay." But Ryan didn't get it.

"Look, I'll show you." After all, he was in training. She neatly cracked open an egg. Letting the yolk slide from one shell to the other, Sarah watched the clear egg white drip into the bowl. "Now, you have to be careful. If you get one speck of yolk into the whites, they won't whip up nice and firm." Finished, she dropped the yolk into the second bowl and set the shells aside. "Your turn."

Looking as if he were diffusing a bomb, Ryan picked up an egg. Sarah stepped back. Hovering might make him nervous. Forehead furrowed, he tapped the egg lightly on the edge of the bowl. Nothing happened.

"Harder." She reached for the egg.

One look from Ryan and she froze. "I've got this, Sarah."

She fell back. When he cracked the egg, she cheered. Maybe she overdid it.

"Is that really necessary?" Sweat beaded on his forehead.

"You're doing great." She zipped her lips. He was still staring at her. "What? What are you looking at?"

Reaching out, he brushed her forehead softly. She felt that touch clear to her toes. "You've got flour in your hair."

"Okay. Thank you." She gave her head a soft shake. The radio played. Ryan cracked eggs. And Sarah wondered what was happening to her.

Just as they were finishing up, her mother popped her head in. "Everything fine back here?" Looking from Sarah to Ryan, Lila gave a perky smile.

"Yep," Sarah said over her shoulder. "Ryan's doing great."

"Oh, goody. The chocolate chip cookies were just snapped up by Cole Campbell. He's taking them over to the PR office for Mercedes and Kate."

"I wonder if Kate brings that baby to work with her." Her friend Kate had given birth to a little boy at the end of August.

"I guess so," her mother said. "Isn't she nursing?"

With that, Ryan wandered back to the ovens.

"Yes, I think she mentioned that. She has a La Leche woman helping her, although I told her to call me any time, especially if she, you know, leaks." Sarah directed her attention to Ryan. "Come back here, you. We have work to do."

Hands on hips, he looked exasperated. "Are you two finished talking about, you know, babies and stuff?"

"Time for me to leave." With a girlish giggle, her mother swirled back to the front.

Sarah turned back to Ryan. They whipped the egg whites. Then, scooping out a spoonful of dough, she rolled it into a ball. "Want to try?"

But she held back a laugh, watching him grab a bit of dough the size of a dime. "Bigger, Ryan. They should all be the same size."

He scooped up a larger lump. "Better, Mom?"

"Fine." Their pace picked up. After rolling all the balls in egg whites and then the pecans, they arranged them on the baking sheets lined with parchment paper. Ryan had preset the temperature and he slid the cookies into the oven.

"So did I pass?" Easing out a breath, he looked relieved—like he'd deactivated that bomb and saved the city.

"We'll know when we taste them. They're buttery and melt-in-your-mouth delicious. I love orange marmalade in the middle but... well, some people prefer strawberry." Her voice trailed off and her eyes fluttered open.

"Jamie." Her brother-in-law's face emptied. "He always spread strawberry jam on his toast."

"He did like strawberry." She bit her bottom lip and, darn it, her eyes filled.

Before she knew it, Ryan was hugging her. "It's okay, Sarah. I miss him too."

"I know you do." She let her head fall upon his chest. For a second she lost herself in the comfort of a shared loss. Beneath her cheek, his heart beat, steady and strong.

But what was she doing? Pushing away, she straightened her apron. Arms falling to his sides, Ryan looked a little stunned himself. "Time to clean up."

"Right." He ran his hands down his apron.

She whisked the bowl to the sink while Ryan sponged off the counter.

Sarah didn't know her brother-in-law that well until Jamie went overseas. Two years behind them in school, Ryan had been the boy who tagged along. Unlike Jamie, he never did that well with his studies. Instead, he drove their parents crazy with his stunts. The motorcycle accident wasn't a surprise. Jamie had warned him plenty of times about driving over the speed limit without a helmet.

Although their mother came from Chicago during Ryan's hospitalization, she was in a new marriage and didn't seem to know what to do. When Ryan was out of danger and on the mend, she left. Sarah had no idea if they'd talked since then.

After Jamie left for Afghanistan, Ryan would show up at The Full Cup or give her a casual call, saying he had something for the boys. The motorcycle accident left him on crutches for a while. She'd invite him for dinner or drop off food at his apartment. But he'd become moody and withdrawn.

"So, gone on any interesting dates lately?" she asked when he was carrying the last pan to the ovens. Stumbling, Ryan caught himself in time to save the thimbles.

"Dates?" Disbelief lifted his voice. Opening the oven, he slid the pan in and then slammed the door shut.

"You know. You pick up the girl and take her to a movie or out for a meal."

The set of his lips told her she was pushing things. "What about you? I don't see you dating."

Sarah didn't expect that. Her heart squeezed tight while the radio played "Jingle Bells." "I just couldn't," she whispered.

Ryan's handsome features folded. "I'm sorry, Sarah. That was a stupid thing to say."

"That's okay, really. I had no right to pry into your private life." Since when had she become his dating service?

"Okay if I leave now?" Already stripping off his apron, Ryan glanced up at the clock.

He wanted to escape. Who could blame him? "Sure. No problem." She felt relieved when the door closed behind him.

Alone in the workroom, Sarah cleaned the bowls and the beaters. When the last batch of thimbles was turning golden, she took them out and dabbed them with preserves—first orange, then strawberry. She'd show Ryan how to do this too. Her mother stuck her head through the swinging door. "Okay if I take a long lunch hour?"

"Sure. No problem." Looked like everyone was cutting out on her. Usually they ate back here together. She enjoyed those cozy, quiet times.

Her mother glanced around. "Ryan gone already?"

"Yes. He left. Didn't even stay to taste a thimble." If her mother took a long lunch hour, Sarah would have to work the front. Maybe the break would be good for her.

Mom left. Sarah took the last pan of cookies from the oven. Going to the front window of the shop, she watched the snow sift over the street. Only a few cars were parked diagonally in front of the shops. After all, it was December, always a slow time. After a hectic summer that had brought love to Lindsay, who had become a close friend, and a beautiful baby boy for Kate Campbell, Sarah should feel happier.

But she didn't expect to feel happy ever again.

The list of Christmas chores played in her head as she stared out at Whittaker Street. She felt so far behind. The boys wanted a train set for Christmas—at least, she thought they did. Maybe she shouldn't have taken them to Tom's Train Store that Saturday after Thanksgiving. But the blinking lights in the window had been hard to ignore. The trains were set up in a separate room, chugging through tunnels, stopping at train stations and tooting at toy people along the way. Miniature trees and houses completed the display. What boy wouldn't want this?

Nathan and Justin had pressed their faces to the glass, transfixed by the magical miniature train whirring around the track. But the train was expensive, from the tiny train station to the coal chute that loaded the car. They must have stayed there at least an hour. What was the harm in dreaming? She had so little to offer this Christmas. Somehow she had to make their Christmas dreams come true.

She was arranging the cheese crowns, brownies and pecan rolls when Mercedes Wheeler passed the front window. Head bent into the wind, she struggled to hold down her blonde hair whipping about the collar of a stylish black cape. No doubt those gloves were real leather. Her years in New York had made Mercedes a fashion plate, although she'd been like that in high school.

The bell above the door jingled as Mercedes swirled inside, bringing a cold blast of air with her. "Wow. It's freezing out there.

And this snow!" With a stamp of her high-heeled boots, she shook off the snow before stepping onto the tile floor.

"Think of it as holiday cheer. We're just beginning the season."

"Don't remind me." Studying the case, Mercedes pointed. "Cheese crown, please. I need my sugar fix."

Grabbing one of her white bakery bags, Sarah slid out the tray and chose a plump pastry loaded with almond frosting. "So how does it feel to be an aunt?"

"Oh, I just love that little guy. Quinn is perfect. I think my sister comes in just to show him off." Mercedes handed Sarah her gold credit card.

"Did Kate enjoy the chocolate chip cookies Cole picked up earlier?"

"Trust me, we devoured them."

"Wait. You can be my taste tester." Only took a minute to dash back and pop three thimbles into a bag. Returning, she handed the bag to Mercedes. "Ryan made these."

"Oh, he did, did he?"

Her friend's sly look made Sarah's face flush. "He's helping us this year."

Mercedes propped an elbow on the high counter. "That boy is seriously hot."

Sarah's cheeks felt as if she were standing in front of an open oven. "Please. He's Jamie's little brother."

With a glint in her eye, her friend said, "Well, I got news, missy. He's all grown up."

Sarah waved her away. "Take your cookies and go."

"Does this mean another two hundred calories?" Mercedes moaned, marching to the door.

"Better you than me." They both laughed.

After Mercedes had scurried back out into the snow, Sarah decided to bring her lunch out front. Sitting at one of the glass topped tables at the window, she opened her ham and cheese sandwich. The snow was picking up. She would have to shovel their little patch of sidewalk. No one would be coming in now and her spirits plummeted.

But maybe she was wrong. A car that looked like her mother's blue Chevy pulled up into one of the spots out front. A blonde stepped out. The wind caught her red paisley headscarf, but she wasn't giving it up.

Time for some fresh coffee and Sarah went back to fill the pot with water. Grabbing a warm thimble, she returned and set the pot to perking. She'd just bitten through the nutty layer of the soft, warm cookie when the door opened. There stood the blonde. Realization turned the thimble to a lump in her throat. Sarah had a hard time swallowing.

"Mom. What have you done to your hair?"

# Chapter 3

Sarah's mother fluffed her pert new hairdo. Gone were the frizzy white curls pinned back with a headband. A sleek blonde wave hung to her mother's chin. "What do you think?"

Sarah struggled to find the right words. "Gosh, Mom. I hardly recognized you."

Her smile slipping, Mom tucked the scarf in her pocket. "Is that a good thing or a bad thing?"

Now she'd made her feel bad. "Forget what I said. You look great, Mom."

"I just thought, after seeing Lindsay's mother at the wedding, that her blonde hair looked so pretty. You know, so young." The last bit was delivered in a whisper.

"So you've been thinking about this for a while?"

Her mother nodded. Sarah had to agree. Rose Wheeler, Lindsay's mom, had been blonde for ages. She did look about ten years younger than Lila. Well, not anymore.

Slipping off her heavy gray coat, her mother looked pleased. "I just thought I'd give myself an early Christmas present."

"You look more like my sister than my mother."

"Oh, nonsense." Her mother couldn't stop smiling. "Phoebe

said to say hello."

"Oh she did, did she?" A member of Sarah's book group, Phoebe owned and operated Gull Harbor's hair salon.

"Guess I'll hang up my coat." And her mother whirled through the swinging half door, humming some Christmas tune.

Had Sarah been too busy starting up her babysitting co-op that she'd missed a change in her mother? Almost thirty, Sarah viewed sixty as mature but not old. Her mother was pretty and still relatively young.

Tying her apron strings, Mom reappeared and peered into the case. "How did your thimbles turn out? You know, the ones you made with Ryan?" Did she give Ryan's name a mischievous uptick?

"Delicious. I could eat all of them. But I won't." Her words were a promise to herself. She was going to fit into her red Christmas dress if it killed her. After all, that dress was tradition. She'd had it since high school, but every year she had to let out the seams a little more.

"The thimbles look so yummy. I have to try them." With that, her mother reached into the case. One little bite had Mom closing her eyes in ecstasy. "These are perfect, sweetheart. So soft and buttery. Maybe Ryan would make a good pastry chef."

"Oh, I don't think cookies are his thing." Resting her chin on one hand, Sarah peered out the window. The lake wind caught the falling snow, shaping ghostlike figures and mini-drifts. "If this blasted snow keeps up, we'll be lucky to sell these today. No one goes out in this kind of weather."

Her mother stopped chewing. "Maybe I should take some to

the library."

Sarah wheeled around. "What? With all this snow?"

Granted, her mother did visit the library every other week. Mildred Wentworth, the head librarian, set new romances aside for her. Of course, that was before Mom's recent interest in ancient history.

"You might get stuck." Sarah didn't want to have to dig Mom's car out of a snow drift. The fact that she'd made it back from Phoebe's salon was amazing...and scary.

"Oh, for goodness sakes. It's just up the highway." Averting her eyes, her mother took another bite. "In weather like this, people like to read. Why not hand out cookie samples?"

With that her mother began to put together one of their white bakery boxes. Then she scooped fresh cookies from the tray. "After all, it's the season to share."

Sarah moaned. "Good grief, Mom. I haven't even started my Christmas shopping."

"No worries," her mother practically sang out. "We have lots of time. Besides, Christmas isn't about presents. It's about people." By this time her mother was back in her coat. She didn't even bother to take off her apron. Shaking out the paisley headscarf, she wrapped it carefully around her new hairdo.

In the past Sarah's mother had been terrified of driving in snow. All that seemed to be a thing of the past. Box in hand she disappeared through the front door, the bell giving a final jingle as she pulled the door shut. Ten seconds later her old Chevy rumbled as she backed out, leaving Sarah at the window.

In the summer, tourists often made The Full Cup their first stop. The women in Sarah's book group visited regularly for cheese crowns and ganache brownies. But today? The only movement on the street was the blowing snow.

Everything was quiet. Too quiet for her.

Time to get to work.

Bustling into the back area, she went to her corner desk and grabbed the recipe binder. The Mexican hot chocolate cookies had been a big success last summer, and she'd ordered a Christmas bell stamp to add a festive touch. Just as she finished mixing the ingredients, her mother returned.

"Your cheeks are as red as my strawberry jam," Sarah said with a laugh. "So what did Mildred think of the thimbles?"

Mom was studying her new hairdo in the mirror next to the bathroom door. Sarah watched with fascination. Lila had never been one to fuss over herself. "Oh, Mildred isn't there."

"Really? Is she sick?"

"Didn't I tell you?" One more pat of approval for the hair. "She took the month off to visit her daughter for the holidays."

"So who's running the place?" Sarah couldn't picture that desk without Mildred's smiling face.

"A substitute." Drifting over to the table, Mom picked up the cocoa and began reading the label. "So, what are you making now?"

"Mexican hot chocolate cookies. Remember how they sold last summer?"

But her mother didn't seem to be paying attention. Hugging the cocoa tin to her chest, she wore a soft smile.

"After I get these going, I thought I'd get things set up for Ryan."

The name snapped Mom from her haze. "So he's coming back?"

"Yes." They'd gone over all this together just last week. "Ryan's working on bread at night and cookies in the morning."

"Wouldn't it be easier to have Ryan all day?"

*Having Ryan all day.* A knot the size of a cheese crown formed in Sarah's throat.

"I needed someone at night," she finally choked out. Well, there it was again. That huge pastry. She cleared her throat. "To handle the bread, you know, since I'm busy with the boys. And you were...." *Getting older.* But she decided not to add that.

"Of course, dear." Her mother began to leaf through the blue binder. "Spritz, chocolate pecan bark, sand tarts. You two will have a great time. Is Ryan happy helping with the Christmas cookies?"

"Your guess is as good as mine. You should have seen him separating the eggs for the thimbles." She smiled, remembering.

Her mother stepped over to the radio and turned up the dial. "I'll be Home for Christmas" was playing. Bing Crosby's soothing voice filled the room. The bell jingled out front and her mother rushed to wait on a customer. Thank goodness someone had come in despite the snow.

Maybe Sarah would save the hot chocolate cookies for tomorrow. It might be fun to watch Ryan work the stamp. Instead, she busied herself with cinnamon rolls. Inhaling the cloves and cinnamon lifted her spirits. Before long, the snow stopped and the scratchy sound of the snow plows came down the street. Good, the streets would be salted by the time she left to pick up the boys.

The bell continued to jingle. Although she couldn't hear the conversations, she thought she heard the word *thimbles*. When she peeked over the swinging door, her mother was talking to a young couple. "You tasted these at the library? Yes, the cookies came from us."

"The thimbles are my husband's favorite," the woman said. "His mother used to make them."

Maybe that trip to the library was worthwhile after all. Returning to her cinnamon roll dough, Sarah finished them off and then began on pecan buns. To her surprise, the front bell kept ringing. After a customer left, she went out front. "I guess your trip to the library paid off."

Her mother gave her a mysterious smile. "Oh, I think so. The library's been busy. Everyone wants to take out a book before the snow starts again."

By the end of the afternoon, the thimbles were gone. Her mother swung through the door with the empty tray. "Will you just look at this?"

"That's amazing." Sarah set the tray in the sink. "I should write a thank you note to the woman taking Mildred's place. What's her name?" Picking up a pen, Sarah grabbed a pad of paper.

Her mother had started wiping down the pan in the sink. "Stuart."

"Must be one of the college interns."

Grabbing a towel, her mother dried the tray with brisk strokes. "Oh, I don't think so." Then she waltzed back to the front of the store, leaving the empty tray and a lot of questions.

Nat King Cole was singing about chestnuts roasting on an open fire. Well, right now Sarah's brain felt roasted. The rumble of Ryan's truck snapped her out of it. The back door opened, bringing a draft of winter air. And there he was with wind-ruffled hair and red cheeks. She smiled.

"Hey, Sarah." Ryan shrugged out of his sheepskin jacket.

"How are the roads? Any trouble coming down Red Arrow?"

"You know Michigan. The crews have been salting the roads since the first snowflake fell." Going straight to the cupboard, he got out the flour and yeast for the bread dough. They were settling into a rhythm. "How did the new cookies go over today?"

"We sold out." Surprise lifted her voice.

Ryan's square jaw dropped. "In this snow? I thought you'd have a quiet day."

He was thinking about her today? Unexpected warmth swirled through her stomach. "Trust me, it's been a day of surprises."

Just then her mother bustled in from the front counter. "The door's locked. I cleaned all the glass counters and table tops. Oh hi, Ryan."

"Wow," Ryan said with a chuckle.

Her mother shot him a coy smile—a look Sarah had never seen before. "You like it?"

"You look beautiful. The hair's great." Ryan looked to Sarah for agreement. "Right, Sarah?"

"Amazing." That was all she could manage.

"Sarah tells me you sold all the cookies we cranked out this morning."

"We did." Her mother gave him the secretive look Justin and Nathan wore after they'd had a pillow fight and left the room a mess.

"Why don't you tell him, Mom?" She wanted to hear her mother's side of the story.

"About what, dear?" Lila was sidling towards the door that led upstairs to her apartment.

"About the cookies. The library." Okay, she was sounding more like an interrogator, not a concerned daughter.

With a dip of her new hairdo, Lila said, "I thought it might be nice to take some cookies to the library. You know, a taste trial."

"Great idea." His back against the counter, Ryan fold muscled arms across his chest. For heaven's sake, he looked like he'd worked in the bakery all his life. Sarah tore her eyes away but not before Ryan caught her staring.

"Those samples sure brought people in." Mom looked to Sarah, who nodded.

"That's terrific. Guess I should get to work." Ryan swung into action and her mother went upstairs.

Sarah had trouble concentrating. You would think a man measuring flour wouldn't appear masculine. But to Sarah's surprise, Ryan did. He handled the bag of flour with authority. Measured the ingredients, narrowing his eyes for accuracy.

"Seems there's a new temporary librarian on staff." She had to tell someone.

"Really?" He started the giant mixer.

Ryan probably didn't visit the library very often. "Mildred Wentworth has been a fixture in that library for as long as I can remember. This holiday season she's gone to visit her daughter in California."

"Good thing they found someone to step in." He mixed the warm water with the yeast. Yep, Ryan had really caught on to this bakery business.

"The temporary librarian's name is Stuart." Sarah wished she'd been more observant. "Now that I think of it, her trips to the library have become more frequent. I mean, who can read four books in two days?"

"Man, I could never do it." Lips twitching, he held up a hand. "Hang on a minute, will you? I have to focus or I'll mess this up."

"I'll just check the shop." Pushing through the door, she did a thorough sweep of the shop out front. Everything was in its place. Mom had always been tidy. Sarah turned off the coffee pot and took a deep breath. Was she making a big deal out of nothing? Probably.

Holding that thought, Sarah returned to the work room where Ryan was shaping mounds of bread dough. "I might stay a bit later tonight."

"Why? You can finish the bread in the morning."

"But don't we have cookies to finish?" Ryan came closer. He smelled of yeast and flour, and they'd never smelled better. "What's up next?"

"Next?" she echoed mindlessly.

He glanced toward the blue binder. "Will we make thimbles again?"

Almost tripping over her feet, she snapped up the recipe. "For starters, tomorrow we'll bake the Mexican hot chocolate cookies."

"What are they?" He looked perplexed.

"The best chocolate cookies you'll ever taste. They're made with cocoa and just a pinch of chili powder." She licked her lips.

His eyes followed. "Sounds great."

"They are." Her grip tightening, she crinkled the recipe in her hand. "I'm sorry, but this day had been upsetting."

"What's wrong?"

"Something's going on with my mother." Her voice ended on a squeak.

"Don't do this to yourself." For a second she thought Ryan might take her in his arms. She could almost feel their warm comfort around her. But instead of reaching for her—and holy moly, hadn't they done that once already today?—he locked his hands together. Muscles twitched in his arms. "So your mom likes the librarian. Can't you just let things roll?"

Her lips trembled. "But what do we know about him?"

Ryan heaved out a breath. "Well, for one thing, he's probably not Jack the Ripper. The guy's a librarian, for Pete's sake."

He had a point. Was that her, cackling? "Oh, Ryan, what would I do without you? You put together the boys' bikes, fixed the leak in the roof, brought me groceries when I had the flu." Sarah dug a tissue from an apron pocket.

"Look, I'm glad to help. I'm, well..." Glancing down at his boots, Ryan seemed to be out of words. He'd never been a big talker. Wisecracks? Sure. Conversation? Not really. Then he tossed his head back. "Why don't you let this thing with your mother slide for awhile? See what happens."

He made good sense. After jabbing at her nose, she tucked her tissue away. "You're right. It's not a big deal."

His brown eyes softened to velvet. "Sarah, you're a good daughter and a great mother."

She never thought she'd hear that from *him*. "If you keep that up, I might cry." Then she noticed the clock. "I have to pick up the boys. I'll leave this recipe here so you can take butter out. You may want to double the batch. Mom might be going to the library again."

She ran for the door and reached for her coat. "See you in the morning?"

"You bet." He was studying the recipe and glanced up. "One more thing. Would it be okay if I take some cookies to Stanley Branson?"

"Well sure." She pulled on her coat. "Let's get these cookies out of here. Otherwise they go straight to my hips."

"I like your hips." The words came fast and so did Ryan's furious blush.

"Why, thank you, Ryan." She could hardly get her gloves on .

They were standing at the back door. The cold air outside battered the old wooden panels. Taking her red scarf that probably matched her face right now, she twirled it around her neck.

"Don't worry so much." Reaching over, Ryan tucked some of her hair under the scarf.

"Okay. Thanks." This guy had never been anything but a thorn in her side. But he just made her feel like she could take on the world. "See you tomorrow."

"Yeah. See ya." He stepped back but he didn't turn away.

Stumbling outside, Sarah hurried to the car, her sturdy shoes crunching in the snow. Then she skidded to a halt, grabbing a door handle to keep from falling. Ryan must have cleaned the snow from her car. The guy was full of surprises.

# Chapter 4

A light was glowing in the back office when Ryan reached Branson Motors later that evening. Did Stanley ever go home? Cutting the engine, he hurried through the cold to the back door, the white box tight under one arm. The smell of chocolate had driven him crazy all the way up Red Arrow. Stamping the snow off his boots, he went inside. Seeing Stanley through the glass of the enclosed office, Ryan hesitated. Was the old man talking to himself? Glasses low on his nose, he sat staring at his computer screen.

Ryan poked his head into the office that smelled of burned coffee. "You working late again?"

"This dang thing." Ripping off the glasses, Stanley rubbed his eyes. "Just getting ready for the end of the year. You know, accounting stuff. Take a load off." He nodded to a chair piled with old newspapers.

The small office was packed with samples, vintage Harley parts, old invoices and yellowing magazines. The pinup calendar might date back to the 80s, along with the worn furniture. A man cave, for sure.

"You'll never win an award for housekeeping." Setting the box on the desk, Ryan transferred the newspapers to the floor and sat down.

"Don't want one." Stanley's eyes zeroed in on the cookies. His nose twitched.

Ryan stretched his legs out. "Man, this feels good." Standing for hours in the bakery left him with a serious back ache. "Don't you leave the books to your accountants?"

"The man who doesn't run the numbers for his own business is a fool. I liked the old paper ledgers, not these fancy computer spreadsheets." Stanley's eyes were still riveted to the box of cookies. In the small enclosed space, the chocolate scent became overpowering. "What have you got there?"

"Just some cookies I baked tonight." Man, this felt girly and weird.

Stanley had that box open in a flash. "You baked these yourself?" Scooping one out, he studied the cookie like it was the new Harley catalogue before biting down. The sounds he made were almost indecent. By the time Stanley finished munching, crumbs were everywhere. Taking one finger, Stanley pressed down on them, one at a time. "Boy, you missed your calling."

Ryan felt pleased. "It's Sarah's recipe. Mexican hot chocolate cookies."

"Kinda got a kick, don't they?" Running a tongue over his teeth, Stanley reached for another.

Getting up, Ryan moved to the desk and leaned over the spreadsheet. "That's what makes them special. You mind if I look at this?"

"Have at it." Stanley pushed his chair away.

"These spreadsheets have some basic formulas."

"Son, you're speaking a foreign language." Getting to his feet, Stanley stepped back. "Can you show me?"

Ryan sat down in Stanley's chair. For the next ten minutes he gave Stanley a quick course in Excel, or what he could remember since high school. By the time he surrendered the chair, the old man looked impressed. "You are a wizard."

"Trust me, I'm not." After jotting down some of the basic formulas, Ryan eased himself back into the chair. "Let me know if you need more help."

Stanley's chair squeaked when he swiveled to face Ryan. He closed the box carefully. "Want to save some of these for later." Then he sat back and studied Ryan, hands folded on his stomach.

Uncomfortable, Ryan squirmed in the chair. The old guy sure had x-ray eyes. "So you start your day early in the morning, work here and then head back to town."

"Ryder said that was okay. I put in at least eight hours here," Ryan reminded him. He didn't want Stanley to think he was goofing off.

"Sounds like you're burning the candle at both ends."

The concern in Stanley's eyes caught Ryan right in the gut. Taking off his belt had been his dad's answer for everything, not that Ryan didn't deserve it. "It's only for three weeks or so. I'm helping Sarah through the holidays."

"So you said." Stanley's lips slowly twisted into a cocky grin. "Well, I hope your efforts are appreciated."

"I think they are." The hug that morning had felt way too good.

For a second there, Ryan almost forgot this was Sarah, the sweetest woman on the planet. "I'm just filling in."

"Uh huh. Why do I think there's more to it than that?"

"What?" Keeping up with his own son had honed Stanley's radar.

"Do you have feelings for Sarah?"

Avoiding Stanley's eyes, Ryan focused on the pricing list posted on the wall. "She's a good woman."

"I know that, son. I've met Sarah. She's fun. Cheerful. The kind of woman who keeps a good house and probably can make a pot roast last for six days. But that's not what I'm asking."

Man, it was hot in here. He opened his jacket. "I don't think of her, you know, romantically." The words felt strange on his tongue.

"Maybe you should."

Ryan's mind drifted back. The soft brown hair that framed Sarah's rosy cheeks. The hands that fluttered when she talked. This was crazy. Just thinking about her made his heart race.

"So you're taken by the widow woman." Stanley was cackling. And there was no other word for it.

Feelings surged through him and Ryan had to clamp them down tight. "Wouldn't do much good, Stanley. Sure I can help in her bakery. Take my nephews go-karting. But..."

"But what?" Stanley looked mystified.

Couldn't the man see? Lurching to his feet, Ryan limped to the door. "Maybe you missed something but I'm a gimp-legged fool. Sarah was married to Jamie—honor roll student, football star and war hero. What would she ever want with me?"

Outside a storm was brewing, rattling the doors on the service bays. After today, he might lie in bed tonight and think of Sarah, all warm curves and sparkling eyes set off by that darn red scarf.

"Ryan, there's a lot more to a man than the way he walks."

"Easy for you to say. I feel like a reject, and I did this to myself." The words cast a familiar gloom over him. "And I'll probably pull something just as stupid in the future."

"Not if you think first. Don't be so hard on yourself." Stanley laced his hands behind his head, staring up at the fluorescent light like it had some answers. "Every man makes mistakes. My wife was a patient woman. Sarah seems like that kind of girl, someone who's interested in more than looks."

"Easy for you to say. Your son can walk into the Rusty Nail and have the attention of every woman in the place without even trying."

Stanley snorted. "Yeah and look where that landed him. He's lucky he got Phoebe back after that one indiscretion. You can be a sour puss but you're not hard on the eyes."

"Thanks, Stanley," Ryan gritted out. "That's real comforting."

"Look, that accident could have been worse. You weren't wearing a helmet and you might have left your face scraped right off on the asphalt."

"I really need to be reminded of that."

Stanley was pleased with himself, like a father who's delivered a speech he'd had stored away. "So it's the limp, is that it?"

He wished the old man would give it a rest. "Yeah. I'm the gimp with a limp."

"No, you're the man who has to learn how to woo a widow." With one leg resting on his other knee, Stanley patted a black boot. "Seems to me you've been punishing yourself instead of looking for solutions. Listen, I know this shoemaker up in St. Joe." And Stanley laid out a plan.

"Is it all right if I take some time off tomorrow?" Ryan asked, slowly digesting Stanley's idea.

"I'll have to ask the boss." Stanley stood up and yawned. "Yep, fine with him. Now I have to drive home to bed and you need a good night's sleep. Courting a widow woman requires energy."

Ryan chuckled all the way up the stairs.

~.~

Sarah barely had time to feed the boys and get them ready for bed. Her book group was coming. Although they'd talked about skipping this month, in the end they decided to bring their favorite cookies and talk about classic Christmas stories. Then no one would have to read a new book. At least that was the plan.

But this group hardly ever stuck to the plan.

"Why do we have to go to bed so early?" Nathan complained as she tucked him in.

"Because Mommy's friends are coming over. And you have school tomorrow."

"You sound just like my teacher." He sounded way older than kindergarten and it broke her heart. "But we're going to see Santa this Saturday, right?"

"You promised," Justin threw in from the other twin bed.

"Yes, Grandma will mind the shop during the Holiday Walk.

And we'll see Santa."

"Good. I've got my list. And so does Justin." Nathan hunched down under his covers.

Sarah's heart sank. How long were their lists? This Christmas she was on such a tight budget. But she wouldn't think about that now.

Tucking the comforter under Nathan's chin, she smoothed the strawberry blonde curls from his eyes. In time the hair would turn chestnut, just like his daddy. Just like Ryan. "Sleep tight, sweetheart. But remember, Santa has a lot of boys and girls to give presents to at Christmas. He can't give children everything on their list."

"Of course he can, Mommy," Justin said with the innocence of a three year-old.

*Don't I just wish.* She gave each boy a kiss. "See you in the morning." After snapping on the night light, Sarah left the door open a crack and scurried downstairs. The girls would be here soon.

She was stacking wood in the fireplace when Chili burst through the door. "Hey, Sarah. Need help?" Toeing off her boots, Chili left them on the brown runner. Then she swirled a plate onto the coffee table, lifting off the foil. "Mexican hot chocolate cookies. Christmas with a bit of spice."

"Thanks. We're making these at the bakery tomorrow." Sarah gave Chili a big hug.

Framed by Chili's dark curls, her friend's brown eyes danced. "You and your *Mamacita*?"

"No, Ryan's helping me."

"Oh, I see." Pulling away, Chili shrugged out of her red parka and walked over to cram it into the front hall closet. The woman was a whirlwind. In addition to raising three kids, she helped her husband Nacho in his produce store on Red Arrow Highway. The place was crazy busy during the tourist season, but in December? Not so much.

"Want to help me start this fire?" That way Sarah could avoid answering questions.

"*No problema.*" Chili got busy wadding up paper and tucking it under the logs. They had the fire going in no time.

The doorbell rang and the door flew open. "Hello, ladies." Bundled up in a blue cape that probably came from her shop Hippy Chick, Diana was next to arrive. "The cook at the care center was making mint brownie bars." She set her plate on the coffee table. "Of course I snatched a few, one of the perks of my position." Diana's husband Will was the administrator of Gull Harbor Care center and they had a great cook.

"I can feel my waistband tightening already," Sarah laughed as she took Diana's cloak.

"Look at this fire!" Sarah's beautiful blonde friend settled in front of the fireplace. Only Diana could look glamorous in a bean bag chair.

"Time to warm our cider. I'll be right back." Sarah disappeared into the kitchen, took a jug of cider from the frig, dumped it into a pan and turned on the stove. Hands on the counter, she caught her breath.

These were her best friends, people who usually made her happy. But this year she had no holiday cheer. Somehow she had to find it. Her boys deserved a fun Christmas. Wasn't that a parent's responsibility?

But she was only one parent.

The doorbell rang again and the front room filled with laughter. Sarah shook herself from gloomy thoughts. Taking out some cinnamon sticks, she dropped them into the cider and added nutmeg and pumpkin spices. While she was stirring the mixture, Kate whirled into the kitchen with her baby Quinn. Such a picture, the two of them together.

"Oh, let me hold him!" Setting down her spoon, Sarah held out her arms. "Isn't he just the most beautiful baby ever? Two or three months now?"

"Three. Can you believe it?" Kate beamed, the proud parent. Sarah remembered when she'd been like that with Nathan. The first baby was always so special.

With sloppy, sweet gurgles, the warm bundle in her arms chased away any holiday gloom. Sarah breathed in the soothing smell of baby powder. "Will you just look at those lashes, that little nose?"

"Nothing about this boy will be little for long." Kate slipped a finger into Quinn's tiny fist and he gripped it tight. The baby gave his mom a gummy smile and Sarah's heart turned over. A sudden surge of longing took her by surprise.

"He'll be all boy," she assured Kate. "Probably tall like his daddy."

"So where is that *vino* you promised?" Chili hollered from the living room.

"Mulled cider," Sarah called back, settling Quinn back in his mother's arms. "Why don't you and the baby get comfortable on the sofa? I'll be right out."

She watched Kate disappear into the other room, Quinn's delicate head cuddled on her shoulder. Yes, Sarah's baby yearning wasn't going away any time soon. But she blocked it from her mind, poured the cider into a pitcher and carried it into the living room. After filling everyone's wine glass, she surveyed the plates of cookies and prayed for restraint, that red Christmas dress on her mind.

Kate had brought lemon bars that her mother had baked. "Mom's all about the baking once the holiday starts."

"But that's Christmas, isn't it?" Sarah offered everyone a poinsettia napkin. "Cookies and traditions. Family and friends." But she choked on the last words.

Reaching over, Kate gave her hand a warm squeeze. "Oh, Sarah."

Clearing her throat, she pushed on. "Ryan and I are filling our shelves with Christmas cookies. See what you think of the thimbles." She motioned to the plate.

"I don't need any more encouragement." Choosing a thimble with a dollop of strawberry jam, Diana bit down and groaned.

"Ry--an?" Chili drew out Ryan's name out in the most indecent way. "So you bake together? You and Ryan?"

"My mother's getting older." But not too old to trek over to the library in snowy weather. "She's working the front counter while I handle the baking."

"With Ry–an." Chili chuckled. "What else is going on in your kitchen, Sarah?"

"Oh, don't be silly." Her cheeks burned. Time for a lemon bar and she scooped one up. The tart taste exploded in her mouth. They'd definitely have to start on these soon for The Full Cup.

"Who is this Ryan?" Diana looking puzzled. A transplant from Chicago, she'd only lived in Gull Harbor for a couple of years. "Have I met him?"

"Tell her," Kate urged. "Tell Diana about Ryan."

Sarah swallowed and took a sip of wine. "Ryan is my brother-in-law. You know, Jamie's brother." Maybe someday it would be easier to say her husband's name.

"A hunk," Kate filled in. "All the girls in Gull Harbor High had a crush on Jamie's little brother."

"Except Ryan was never little." Chili chortled. "*Que hombre!* Tall with big shoulders." She held her hands wide. With a gulp, Sarah could almost see Ryan filling that space. The heat from the crackling fire was getting to her.

"Ryan always had that attitude," Kate said, tracing her baby's face with one finger. Quinn smiled up at her, waving a fist. "He was a bad boy."

"But that accident. *Terrible.*" Chili shivered. The motorcycle crash had shocked everyone.

"His leg is fine now," Sarah was quick to say. "I don't think he rides that Harley anymore. Ryan's changed a lot."

"You hardly notice the limp," Kate said.

"Makes him more macho, no?" Chili wiggled her eyebrows.

What a relief when the doorbell rang and Phoebe barreled in, cheeks flushed from the cold. "Oh my gosh. It's freezing out there."

"How was the driving?" Jumping up, Sarah helped Phoebe off with her jacket and tucked it in the closet.

"Not bad. Roads were salted." She rubbed her hands together, squishing onto the sofa and cooing over Quinn. "I want one of these in my Christmas stocking."

"I think Ryder can help you with that," Chili teased. But Phoebe said nothing.

"Phoebe, do you know this Ryan guy who's working at Sarah's coffee shop?" Diana asked.

"You mean the coffee shop that's really a bakery?" Phoebe chuckled. "Don't take that the wrong way, Sarah."

But Sarah was used to the teasing.

"Yes, I know Ryan," Phoebe said, watching Quinn curl a tiny hand over her finger. "He's renting the apartment above Branson Motors."

"Ah, the inside story," Chili cooed while the others laughed.

During a lively discussion of Ryan's assets, she wondered who they were talking about. "Ryan is Jamie's little brother."

"Not much younger." Quinn started to fuss and Kate jiggled him in her arms. "Guess it's feeding time." Draping a diaper over one shoulder, Kate began to nurse. The beautiful picture deepened Sarah's yearning.

"Why are we even talking about age?" Kate said, smiling down at the baby. "Carolyn's dating a man who is ten years younger. Brody doesn't seem to mind a bit."

They all laughed. "I miss having Carolyn around," Sarah said quietly. "It was so good to see her last summer. Do you think she'll ever move back to Gull Harbor?"

"From Santa Fe and Brody?" Diana asked, her brows arching. "I doubt it. She's landed a teaching position and loves it. But she might visit over the holidays."

"Back to Ryan." Chili waved her glass of cider. "Is he dating anyone?"

Sarah shook her head with what she hoped looked like sisterly concern. "Can't we fix him up with someone?"

The room fell silent. All eyes swung toward Sarah. "What? What did I say?"

"Why not you?" Kate hooted just as Quinn burped.

Chili shot her a sly look. "Sounds like you two are hitting it off."

"But not like that." Heat rolling from her neck to her cheeks, Sarah moved the rocker away from the heat. "That's crazy, Chili."

"Why?" Kate wasn't buying it.

"He's Jamie's little brother, that's why. Ryan's been a great help to me but...no."

Finally, the conversation moved away from Ryan. The women chatted like the old friends that they were and never got to the Christmas stories. Sarah popped in some Christmas CDs and strains of Nat King Cole singing about chestnuts roasting on an open fire filled the room.

After her friends had left, Sarah cleaned up the kitchen and went to bed. Taking Jamie's photo from her nightstand, she propped it up on her knees. So handsome, her husband.

"The boys are doing so well. Nathan and Justin will have a wonderful Christmas. I'll see to that." No way would she share her concerns about Nathan and his moods.

"I had book group tonight, and the girls teased me about Ryan. Can you imagine? I would never think of your little brother in that way. He's doing great with the baking, though. You'd be proud of him. Maybe Ryan's turned over a new leaf."

Her voice echoed in the lonely bedroom. Sarah didn't know what else to say. Kissing her fingertips, she pressed them to Jamie's confident smile. The glass felt cold beneath her fingers. "Good night, honey." She set the photo back on her nightstand.

After she turned off the light and snuggled down under her quilt, Sarah couldn't fall asleep. Images of Ryan clouded her mind.

And it wasn't in a sisterly way.

# Chapter 5

The ride down Red Arrow this morning had been cold and dark. But remembering Stanley's expression when he chowed down on the cookies last night made Ryan smile. Once inside the warm back room, Ryan tied on an apron and got to work. Sarah wouldn't be here for three hours and he wanted to surprise her. Pulling her pastry dough from the refrigerator, he set it next to the bread dough.

He was trying. Really trying.

*I'm helping you out this Christmas, Jamie.*

Helping Sarah out. Maybe Stanley was right. Maybe all his time at The Full Cup was more than work. On the way down he wasn't thinking about cookies or bread. No, Sarah's sweet smile was on his mind. The way her hair fell to her shoulders in soft curls when she took off the hair net. The feathered eyebrows that he wanted to trace with his fingers.

This was crazy. *Back to work.*

He needed caffeine bad. The front room was cool and dark until he flipped on the lights. In no time he had the coffee perking out front. Studying the family-size pot, Ryan had some ideas about the whole coffee issue—if he ever had the nerve to talk about them with Sarah. After all, her dad had named the place The Full Cup, but they didn't sell that much coffee. The coffee could be a money maker, but Sarah and her mom hardly ever pushed the flavored espresso.

Back at the butcher block table, Ryan smiled as he worked, imagining what Stanley would say if he could see him. This place was such a switch from Branson Motors, where the smell of oil hung heavy and the clang and grind of tools made your ears ring. The other guys told jokes he could never repeat, not here anyway. If he were truthful, Ryan liked this back room a lot better.

Quiet surrounded him. No movement yet in the apartment upstairs. Sarah would be here after she took Nathan to school and Justin to the playschool she'd started. He missed her on the day she didn't come in because she had the kids at her place.

*He missed her?* His hands stopped the rhythmic pulling of the dough.

Really? Ryan didn't want to think about it.

And he didn't have time. The clock reminded him he had a schedule. He set the dough to rise and got on with it.

Grabbing the blue binder from the shelf, he leafed through it. Clippings and scrawled recipes fell to the floor. He scooped them up. Some were probably written by Sarah's father. Others were in Jamie's handwriting, including one for beer and raisin muffins. *Future* was scrawled across the top. But Jamie hadn't been granted that future. Ryan tucked it back inside.

Finally he found the brownies. Sarah probably had this one in her head, but he knew zip about baking. Scanning the ingredients, he figured he could handle it. Chopping nuts? No way would he cut corners by dumping the bag of walnuts into Sarah's blender. No sir. She liked her walnuts in chunks "so people can taste their goodness." He had no idea what she was talking about but he grabbed the knife. Before long he had two pans of brownies in one oven and was shaping bread dough for the other. Multitasking like crazy, he hardly noticed when the darkness outside turned to the cold gray of dawn.

The door opened and Sarah whirled through. "My oh my," she said with a smile. "Do I smell chocolate?" She unwound the scarf and hung up her coat. "What have you been up to?"

That had to be the first time someone had asked that without expecting an apology. "Thought I'd get things going."

Her eyes traveled to the cooling racks. "Will you look at this? You've already finished the brownies." Now, some women at the Rusty Nail put a lot of goop on their eyes. A lot of guys went for that. Not him. He'd take Sarah's sparkling eyes without any makeup any day.

She turned to another tray. "And are these the Mexican hot chocolate cookies?" You'd think she'd just discovered gold.

Suddenly bashful, he tucked his hands in his jean pockets. "Yeah. Thought I'd try them last night. Seemed to turn out okay. Stanley thought they were great."

"And you used the stamp on the top?" Pulling out a tray, she studied each detail.

Now wasn't the time to mention it had taken him four tries to get that darn bell design right on the top. "Yep. Don't worry. I washed it and put it back in your drawer."

"Oh, Ryan, you're the greatest." Sarah's arms came around him from the back and squeezed. Soaking in the warmth of her body, he didn't move. He had to remind himself that this was his sister-in-law. Sweet Sarah. The woman who'd never wanted anything to do with him. But his body hadn't gotten the message. When she laid her head against his back, he could almost feel his bones melt.

Taking his hands from his pockets, he didn't know what to do. So he patted the hands locked around him. Ryan's heart was thumping like the kettle drum in the Fourth of July Parade. "You're welcome."

Suddenly her hold sprang loose.

Ryan turned. Sarah came up to his chin, but she wasn't looking up. Her arms were locked across her chest, knuckles white from the pressure. He wished she'd say something. Maybe she could sense the thoughts galloping through his head. "Sarah?"

"Sorry," she whispered, eyelashes feathered on her cheeks.

He lifted her chin. "About what?"

"I shouldn't have done that. It was silly."

Disappointment deflated him. "No it wasn't. It showed that you appreciate me, I guess."

"Oh, I do." She lifted troubled eyes. "I really do."

"Then what's wrong? Did I goof up somewhere?" That was the story of his life.

The timer sounded. Reluctantly, he limped off to sweep the loaves of bread from the oven. As usual, his hip ached from all the walking back and forth. At the garage, he stayed in one place as much as possible.

No matter how busy he got, today he was traveling to St. Joe to visit the shoemaker Stanley had mentioned.

A door closed upstairs and Lila came down the steps, yawning. It would take a while for him to get used to that blonde hair, not that she'd didn't look pretty with it. "How was book club, Sarah?" she asked.

"Oh, fine." Sarah was cutting the brownies into neat squares, but her knife seemed to wiggle a bit.

"Tell me again, which book did you read?" Lila tied an apron around her.

Even though Ryan was busy sliding the hot trays onto the cooling racks, he didn't miss the blush in Sarah's cheeks.

"The truth is, we didn't really get around to the books." Sarah's voice trailed off.

"That's too bad." Lila leaned over the brownies and sniffed. "My, these smell wonderful."

Okay, Ryan was curious. "If your book group didn't talk about books, what did they talk about?"

"Just stuff." Finished cutting her squares, Sarah studied them.

Lila's eyes darted between Sarah and Ryan. "Ohhhh."

*Oh, what?* Women were a mystery. He shoved a sheet of sour dough bread into the oven.

"So what are you two up to today?" Lila's eyes sparkled. "I mean, anything new on your baking schedule, Sarah?"

"Lemon bars. Kate brought some last night." Turning to the blue binder he'd left open, she paged through. "Here we go.

Lemon bars." She smoothed a hand over the page. How did such delicate hands get so much work done?

"I'll just leave you to it," her mother said, disappearing through the swinging doors.

"Any eggs that have to be separated today?" he asked, hoping to heck she said no.

"No eggs to separate, just lemons to peel. I picked up a bag full from Nacho's vegetable market yesterday but I left them in the car." Sarah's eyes darted to the door. "Hope they're not frozen stiff."

"I'll get them." Ryan needed some air. Not bothering with a jacket, he rushed out to her car. The sharp cold air reminded him of February when the boys dared each other to hop in the lake to prove how strong they were. They'd been idiots back then.

Slipping on the hard-packed snow, he opened her car, grabbed the bag of lemons and dashed back inside.

"Thank you, Ryan." Slitting the bag open with her knife, Sarah squeezed one. "Nah. They seem fine."

Now, how did she know that? The woman was just plain amazing.

While she got busy measuring out the flour and sugar, Ryan took the hot chocolate cookies out to Lila, who fussed over them. He felt pretty pleased about that. Then he hustled back to watch Sarah work. Sometimes she'd talk to herself, saying stuff like, "Just a little bit" or "even it off perfectly." She'd get this cute little frown between her eyes.

"What can I do to help?" After all they weren't paying him to stand here like a goof staring at Sarah.

Opening one of the wide drawers below the counter, Sarah whisked out a metal thing that looked dangerous. "Now with grating, we're just whisking off peels. Not too hard. Just lightly take off the thick yellow skin."

He leaned in, the lemon tickling his nose. "Smells good."

She smiled. "Kind of gets to you, doesn't it?"

"Yep, you do." What had he just said? "I mean *it* does."

But Sarah hadn't heard him. She was laying into those lemons when all of a sudden she yelped. The grater clattered to the chopping board. "Oh, I am such an idiot." She peered down at her bleeding knuckles.

He grabbed her hand. Blood was seeping through tiny nicks in her delicate skin and he felt nauseous. "You're not an idiot but we need some bandages."

"In the medicine chest above the sink. What would the health department think if they ever saw me, bleeding into my cookies?" she joked in a wobbly voice.

"They'd probably ask for one." Ryan was off to the bathroom. Only took him a second to find the box. The only bandages he saw were from the Avenger movies. Sarah must use these for the boys. Grabbing the box, he headed back, painfully aware of how his uneven walk must look as he covered that open stretch of floor.

"Hold still." Ryan told her, tearing a bandage from its paper wrapping with his teeth. "You'll need one for each knuckle." He was winding the third bandage around her middle finger when Sarah's mother spun in from the front.

"Oh my goodness." Stopping in her tracks, Lila gave them a look. Jolted, Ryan dropped Sarah's hand.

"Mom, look at how careless I am." Sarah wiggled her fingers while Ryan closed the metal box with a snap. "What is it?"

"Oh, nothing," Lila said in a high, sing-song voice. The bell jingled in the shop and she dashed back to the front.

Ryan didn't want Sarah's mom to be getting any ideas, not that he wasn't beginning to have plenty of his own. "Why don't you measure and I'll grate?"

"Think you can handle it?" Sarah flexed her fingers.

"Of course I can." Ryan picked up a lemon. How hard could this be?

He laid into it. Hard. The darn lemon wouldn't budge. It was stuck.

"You're not digging to China." Sarah laughed after he'd finally gouged a chunk out of the lemon. How was she getting those itty bitty peels? "Ease up."

That wasn't easy for him but it worked. Pretty soon he had the light strokes down. In his mind he was skimming Sarah's soft skin. Barely touching it while he hummed along to "I'll be Home for Christmas." While he grated, Sarah cut and squeezed the lemons. "Do you think the lemon bars will sell out like the thimbles?" he asked.

"They might, if my mother visits the library again." Lowering her voice, Sarah said, "I wonder how serious this thing is with the librarian."

He couldn't help but smile. "How long has she been alone?"

"Almost ten years now." Sarah's voice held a wistful note. Was she thinking of her own situation?

"Sounds like it's high time, right? I mean, for your mother."

"Time for what?" She stared at him blankly.

Head down, he kept scraping. "It must get lonely for her, Sarah."

She didn't say anything for the longest time. "Yes, very lonely," she finally whispered.

Her words opened up a whole world of hurt. He set down the grater and wiped his hands on a towel. "This will get better, Sarah. With time."

"Isn't it awful?" She lifted eyes filled with tears. "But I don't want to forget him."

"You never will." He thought about his brother every day. Every time Ryan hit a pothole along Red Arrow, Jamie came to mind. They used to alert each other with a text. "You don't forget people who've been so important in your life. But I guess, like your mom, you move on. You have to."

Eyes red, Sarah crinkled her apron in her bandaged fingers.

He wanted to comfort her.

*Don't even think about it.*

Instead, he picked up the grater. Pulling a tissue from her apron, she dabbed at her nose. "Guess we'd better get busy. I want to bake a new batch of thimbles too."

"Again?" The thought of separating eggs again made him drop the grater.

"Rinse that off before you use it again," Sarah told him in a crisp tone.

"Sure thing, boss lady."

"Puh-lease." Her laughter followed him to the sink. For the next two hours they turned out cookies and pastries. Then it was time for him to head to the garage.

He was putting on his coat when she said. "Are you coming to the Holiday Walk this Saturday?"

"Yeah. I told Cole I'd step in for him as Santa this year." Ryan tried to inject some enthusiasm into his voice. He wasn't looking forward to it.

"You'll make a great Santa."

"I couldn't say no. He's so busy with the new baby and all."

"Being Santa will get you into the holiday spirit."

"Ho, ho, ho." He felt as grim as that sounded. "You always see the bright side, Sarah."

"I try." She trailed him to the door, as if she was sorry to see him go.

When he cracked open the door, the cold blast of air made Sarah shiver. "Get inside. You'll freeze."

She waved good-bye and closed the door. Ryan climbed in the truck. Giving a lazy groan, the engine didn't want to turn over. But on the third try, it started. He bumped over some icy patches in the alley and finally made it out to the street. But all the way up Red Arrow Highway, the warmth of the bakery stayed with him. Working together felt good. There was nothing phony about Sarah and he liked that.

Then he hit a pothole. *Got that, Jamie? Help me out here.*

Maybe being with his sister-in-law was getting way too comfortable.

~.~

Nathan and Justin were giddy with excitement Saturday morning. Sarah suspected they'd been sneaking cookies from the store. More than once lately she'd found crumbs under their pillows. Maybe Mom was the culprit. Sometimes she felt that her mother tried to fill the loss of their dad with sweets.

But sugar wouldn't do it. And it wouldn't help Nathan behave. Friday he'd brought home a note from his teacher. Nathan had shoved some other boy over something, and Sarah had to call Monday.

But she wouldn't think about that now. On Saturdays, she worked out front while the boys played quietly in the back. But today Santa was arriving at noon. As usual, Sarah was running late. Maisy Bows had come in, breathless because she was having a children's party after the Holiday Walk and needed cookies. The platter took a little time, so now Sarah had to rush.

"Come on, boys." She helped them zip up their jackets. "You don't want to miss Santa."

"I'm trying to remember my list," Justin said so seriously that she had to smile. Finally, they were both dressed in jackets, hats, warm scarves and mittens.

Out in the shop, her mother was ringing up customers. Sarah would have to check to make sure the coffee dispenser was full. The pot of coffee she kept in a corner near the window was free for anyone but she charged for the espresso drinks. Mom always encouraged shoppers to take the free coffee. "That crazy machine with all the levers was your father's idea."

Word was that a national coffee company was sizing up Gull Harbor, with the intention of opening a shop. Sarah didn't like to think about it.

This would be a big day for the shop. The Holiday Walk drew folks from the nearby towns. Ryan had helped her stock the display case. They'd been busy since they opened at eight.

"Be back soon," she mouthed to her mother over the head of Lisa McGill, who was choosing pastries for her next ladies club meeting.

Outside, the sidewalk was packed. Children clung to their parents' hands or huddled in their arms. The crowd peered down the street, hoping that Santa would appear soon. Usually six boys from the high school dressed as Santa's reindeer to pull the sleigh.

People greeted her as Sarah led Nathan and Justin through the crowd, but she was on a mission. The line for Santa formed early. Christmas carols poured from the speakers placed along the street. Impatient, the boys tugged her along. She hoped she could get back to the shop soon to help her mother. With such cold weather, people might want gingerbread or eggnog coffee and that would throw Lila into a tizzy.

"Sarah! Over here!" Phoebe waved and Sarah steered the boys in her direction.

"How do you like your mother's hair?" Phoebe bubbled. "I forgot to ask you at book club."

"She looks so different," Sarah admitted. "Younger. You're a miracle worker."

"I thought she needed something. You know, since she has that new guy and everything."

"She told you about him?" The shock must have shown on her face.

"Oh, dear. Me and my big mouth. I didn't know it was a secret." Phoebe's face flushed darker than her red hair. "She didn't tell you about the new guy at the library?"

"Oh, him. Sure." Her suspicions growing, she waved a casual good-bye. "Gotta run, Phoebe. Have to line up for Santa."

Sarah's head whirled as she led the boys through the crowd. She felt hurt. Mom was holding out on her. Finally they joined the other parents at the end of the street where Santa's chair was set up. A brisk wind from the lake lifted her hair and waves battered the ice floes along the shore. But at least the sun was shining brightly, reflecting off mounds of snow.

Kate Campbell and her husband Cole approached with baby Quinn bundled on Cole's back. "Look at you! Quinn's first Christmas." She gave Kate a quick hug. Cole's daughter Natalie was with them, cooing over her baby brother. They made a perfect family.

"Maybe I'll ask Santa for a baby, Mom," Justin said when Kate and Cole turned to talk to some of their neighbors.

"Justin, that's stupid," Nathan threw his little brother a sharp look.

"Now that's not nice, Nathan," Sarah said. "We all have our own Christmas wishes."

Nathan pressed his lips together. But when she turned to scan the street for Santa, she heard him whisper, "That's not what we need, Justin."

In the distance came the faint sound of jingle bells. A hearty "Ho, ho, ho" fell over the crowd with welcoming cheer.

"It's Santa, Mommy." Justin jumped up and down. His older brother watched the sleigh approach, a determined look in his eye.

Sarah sure hoped they didn't recognize Ryan's voice.

Perched high in the sleigh, Ryan felt like an imposter. He was also having the time of his life. The pine branches tucked in the sleigh sent out an intoxicating smell. Happy faces turned up toward him and excitement filled the air. Right in the center stood Sarah with Nathan and Justin. How he wanted to make their Christmas something special. Last night in his barren apartment he'd practiced dropping his voice so the two boys wouldn't know he was Santa.

As he waved and smiled at all the little faces, a bit of the Christmas spirit worked its way into his heart. This was what the season was all about. Sharing love and happiness. At the end of the street his nephews' faces glowed with excitement. Although this costume weighed a ton and the white beard had been tricky, he was glad to be here. His throat was feeling scratchy from calling out, "Ho, ho, ho!" in a deep voice.

The sleigh circled and he stepped down. A high back chair draped in red stood in front of some pine trees. Sitting down, he adjusted his cap. Dressed as elves with bells bobbing on their caps, two high school girls coaxed children toward him. The line began to move. The smaller children sat on his knee while older kids stood. Some took out a list. With the exception of a little girl who burst into tears and was bundled away by her dad, the children were really into this.

The lists were similar, he soon learned, depending on the age. The younger kids wanted play action figures or Frozen dolls. If they were older, electronic iPads and iPhones, drones and robots topped their list. Some drilled down to model numbers, which was hilarious.

Then Cole stepped up with his little girl Natalie. "And thank you, Santa, for visiting Gull Harbor today," Cole said pointedly. Hah. The guy was just relieved that Ryan had said yes or he'd be the one in the suit that felt hotter than one of the ovens. Cole's daughter Natalie ticked things off on her gloved fingers while her father rolled his eyes.

"And a new iPad with a hot pink cover," she concluded.

With a parting wave, Cole led his family away. Kate and Cole were such a great couple. Sarah had told him the two had been together in Debate Club in high school.

Ryan adjusted his cap. The winter sun blazed, hotter than he'd imagined. As he welcomed the next child, Ryan kept one eye on Sarah talking to the women in front of her. She could probably win the prize as Miss Congeniality of Gull Harbor. While the other children jumped up and down and chattered with excitement, Nathan and Justin had a solemn concentration about them. He began to sweat big time. Finally, his nephews stepped up.

Showtime. "Ho, ho, ho! And what have we here? Are you two twins?"

"We're not twins," Nathan said dismissively. "We're brothers. I'm the oldest." The boys did not sit on his knee. They stood like the older kids, and that tore off a little piece of Ryan's heart. But he had a job to do.

"And what would you like under your tree?"

Drawing closer, they looked cautiously over their shoulder at Sarah. "We don't want our mom to hear," Nathan whispered.

"I can fix that." Ryan motioned to Sarah. "Can you wait over by the tree. Santa has his secrets." He pointed to a tree at the end of the group of pines. Not looking happy, Sarah edged back.

"You see, here's the thing," Nathan began. "We lost our dad." His voice broke and another chunk of Ryan's heart ripped away.

Justin picked up. "Yeah, we need a daddy. Mommy says ours is not coming back 'cause he's our heavenly hero now."

He never saw this coming. Gutted, Ryan wet his lips. "Your dad must have been a very good man. I'm sure he felt bad about leaving you, but heroes have a job to do." What was he rambling about?

"Heroes give up their lives so that all families can be free." Nathan rattled off. Ryan would bet a hundred bucks Sarah had used those words with the boys more than once. What a load she carried.

"....so we want Uncle Ryan."

*Wait. What?* Bending, he drew closer to the boys. "You want this Uncle Ryan to do what?" If they had an expectation, then he wanted to meet it.

"We want Uncle Ryan to marry our mom so we have him for a dad," Nathan said with maddening practicality.

"Nobody else," Justin added, stabbing one mittened hand into the other. "He's the one."

*The one?* Was Sarah seeing other men? The waiting families were getting restless.

"Got it. I mean, Santa tries very hard to make all Christmas dreams came true." He gulped. "Anything else you'd like?"

Both boys shook their heads. The elves waited with a little girl. Nathan and Justin walked away with their shoulders squared. They looked proud, like they'd finished the job. He remembered the year he and Jamie picked apples in their grandmother's orchard. She wanted a bushel. They gave her three. That's how the kids looked. Like they'd accomplished something.

He blinked furiously. "Are you okay?" One of the elves asked, leading a little girl in a green jacket toward him.

He stabbed at his damp eyes with a red mitten. "This moustache is driving Santa crazy."

By the time two o'clock came, Ryan had lost his voice. The reindeer dragged the sleigh to storage at the North Pole. Then he had to hightail it back to the bakery. Lila had offered him her apartment to change. He had an appointment up in St. Joe at the shoemaker's shop and they closed at four because of their own holiday walk.

Fumbling with the glossy black buttons, he wanted to rip off the Santa suit. The expressions on his nephews' faces stayed with him. Why had they chosen him?

Sarah deserved a better man. Not a goof-off who'd spent most of high school smoking in back of old man Johnson's farm. A guy who'd been so crazy that he'd taken a bet to race down Red Arrow and nearly killed himself.

A new heel on his boot wouldn't matter. He was not the man for Sarah and her boys.

# Chapter 6

Ryan spent Sunday walking. His boots felt level on the pavement and that was amazing. Since he didn't want to bump into anyone he knew, he walked the streets of St. Joe. The extra height in the right heel made a huge difference. Striding along, he checked out Christmas windows, especially toys for Nathan and Justin. The December wind ruffled his hair and bit his ears. He couldn't wait to see Sarah.

Monday he arrived at The Full Cup earlier than usual. After hanging up his jacket and turning on the ovens, he walked. Worn by age, this wooden floor could be tricky. Still, his boots struck the boards with confidence, and he loved the sound of his heels on the wood.

Then he got to work. The air filled with that yeasty smell he'd grown to like. When the loaves were ready, he started shoving them into the oven. Then he worked on the pastries. He'd watched Sarah enough times now that he knew what to do. The cheese crowns were the first to go in, followed by cinnamon buns. Not knowing what Sarah's plans were for the day, he set out plenty of butter for cookies. As he worked, he listened for her car.

But when she finally arrived, she barely looked at him. "Hey,

Ryan. How are you doing today?" She slammed the door shut behind her.

"Fine." He sidled closer, pivoting a little on his boots. "Are you all right?"

"Of course. Why?" Ripping off her scarf, she hung it up.

"No reason." His question seemed to offend her.

Tension had a hold on Sarah's pretty face. Hardly pausing for breath, she began to rattle off instructions. "Business was great Saturday, but customers emptied the racks. We've got to get going." Pressing a hand to her forehead, she looked upset. Her red-rimmed eyes were accented by her pale skin. Had she even slept last night?

"Whoa, whoa," he said, stepping closer. "Slow down, Sarah."

"I can't. Not when there's so much to do." Ripping off her coat, she missed the hook on her first try.

"Let me help. Everything will be fine." Ryan lifted her heavy winter coat from the floor and hung it up

"Thanks, Ryan." Tension rolled off her body as she slipped into her apron and pulled on her hair net. "We have to bake sand tarts, lemon bars, thimbles and maybe even gingerbread men today."

Then she sniffed. "Have you started the pastries?"

"Done." He wanted Sarah to know she could count on him.

"Oh, good. Great." Her shoulders eased a bit. But she still didn't really look at him as he strolled between ovens and the cooling racks. Instead she checked the butter.

Ryan finally gave up. "Where do you want me to start?"

"Sand tarts. You know where the pecans are."

Okay, so she wasn't going to notice. *Get over yourself.* But he wanted to know what was bothering her. He got to work chopping, zesting, sifting and measuring.

Last week when they worked together, he'd enjoyed seeing her face flush from the heat, laughed when she ended up with flour on her nose or cheek. And while they worked, she chattered. He liked the sound of her voice more than what she was saying.

But this morning she was quiet and worrying.

"Nathan's acting up in school. He brought home a note. I have to call Mrs. Wilcox today."

"Can't they cut the kid some slack?" He took out a tray of rye bread. If he had a dollar for every time his mother had to call a teacher, he'd be a rich man. "This is a rough year for him...and you."

"Sure, they know it's because of Jamie. But what can I do about that?" Her voice caught. He felt helpless. The boys missed their dad.

"What did they say they wanted for Christmas?" Sarah pinned him with her eyes. "Why did you make me move away? I couldn't hear."

Now, this was a hard one. "Just the usual stuff. I can't remember. There were so many kids that day." He jammed the tray of bread onto the cooling rack.

"I suppose so." Her expression clouded. "You were awfully busy."

Nathan and Justin were his only nephews. No way would he not remember their Christmas list. But he could never tell her.

Ryan thought back to his own childhood toys. "Trains. I think they mentioned trains."

Sarah's eyes brightened. "I did take them to the train shop. What's so secret about that?"

The bread timer went off. How could he explain why he couldn't tell her? Opening the oven door, he grabbed a pan with his bare hands. Pain seared him. The pan teetered on the edge of the rack.

One look at his face and Sarah grabbed the red mitts and transferred the pan to the cooling rack. He just stood there, feeling like an idiot. "Are you all right?"

Shaking off the mitts, she faced him. Ryan had to drop his gaze. He didn't want her to know that his hands felt like they'd been thrust into hot coals.

"Cold water." She nudged him over to the sink.

"Don't know what I was thinking." Now, that was a lie. All he thought about was her.

"Just an accident. I've done the same thing." She turned on the cold water.

Standing next to the old sink, he let the water flow over his hands.

"What is it?" Sarah said briskly. "This isn't like you. What's on your mind?"

"I guess it's just the whole Christmas thing." He grabbed a towel and Sarah turned off the faucet. Ryan should be better at lying. He'd had plenty of experience.

"You're thinking of your brother, aren't you?" Sarah's own eyes filled. "Oh, Ryan. Don't think I don't feel the same. Both me and the boys."

The emptiness in her eyes only made his own pain worse. It killed him to even bring this up, but he wanted the best for her. And that wasn't him.

"Have you ever thought of dating, Sarah?"

"No way." Grabbing a sponge, she wiped down the butcher block counter with jerky strokes. "I can't even think of it."

Taking the sponge from her hands, Ryan set it on the sink. He was no good at talking about feelings. "The boys might need a man around the house."

Sarah looked at Ryan as if he'd lost his mind. Maybe he had. The thought of having another man play ball with his nephews or take them to movies made his head hurt. Maybe he should suggest some limits. "Of course, I'd want to check him out first."

The hurt in her eyes turned to outrage. "Oh you would, would you?"

Shuffling in his boots, Jamie nearly lost his footing. What right did he have to say something like that? "I just want you to be careful. That's all, Sarah."

The words felt like chunks of dry bread in his mouth. He wasn't any good at this. Jamie had been the one who always said the right thing. His older brother could be clever and kind at the same time. Not Ryan. He laid out whatever was on his mind like a slab of meat at Froehlich's Butcher Shop.

Sarah was studying him and her eyes softened. "I know you mean well, Ryan. You're always here for us. Thank you for that."

She lay one cool hand over his.

The light touch of her skin zinged through his body. "I'm h-happy you think of me like that. Dependable, I mean."

Years ago, she never would have said that he was there for her. He was the pain in everyone's side. The black sheep of the family. His behavior caused too many calls from the principal. Too many complaints from neighbors that he'd busted their fence or taken all their ripe cucumbers or done donuts in their fields with his pickup. Back then he'd found his stupid pranks hilarious.

Now he wished he could punch the reset button. For her.

Blood pounded in his temples from holding back. Sarah smelled like almonds from mixing the sand tarts. How easy it would be to wrap his arms around her. Whisper words in her hair that would probably horrify her.

She gave her apron a tug over the full figure he found enticing. "We're fine. I'm, well, everything's fine. So the boys really said trains?"

Nodding slowly, he swallowed hard. No way could he reveal what the boys had asked for without looking like a fool. Time to change the subject. "Do you mind if I ask you a business question?"

"Sure. Ask away."

"Why do we focus on baked goods when the shop's named The Full Cup?" He really pulled that one out of the air. But he had been wondering.

Her surprised laughter filled his ears and his heart. "Good question. My dad named the business. He thought flavored coffees would be the future. Mom liked to bake but Dad pictured a cozy coffee shop, maybe with some bakery. The fancy machine my father bought was way beyond Mom. She gave him a hard time because 'that contraption' cost a lot of money."

Ryan chuckled. "Your dad had a point. Espresso coffees go for a pretty price."

"I know that. But Mom still hates that machine. She doesn't know how to work it." Her curls had escaped the net. Frowning, she played with one, and he could almost feel it tickle his burned hand. "The flavored coffees take time. I can't be in the front working the machine and in the back baking too."

Ryan couldn't let this drop. He also couldn't stop staring at that curl. "I understand. But still..."

"What's that smell?" Sarah sniffed and ran to the wall of ovens.

The cheese crowns. What else could go wrong? While he stood here dreaming about soft curls, the cheese crowns had become charcoal briquettes.

"I'm so sorry, Sarah." Clumsy as usual, he had trouble pulling the baking mitts over his burned hands.

But Sarah was on it. She had the trays out in a second. "Oh, dear." Her face fell as she stared at the charred edges of the pastries.

"I'll do another batch."

Her eyes swirled to the clock. "No problem, Ryan. We can live one day without them. Let's get to work on the cookies, okay?"

But it wasn't okay. Not for him.

~.~

By the time Ryan left that day, lemon bars, thimbles and sand tarts filled the case, just in time for the lunch crowd. Sarah felt so bad about his burned hands. He didn't seem himself today, although his question about the coffee got her thinking. Her mother would have to buy into it and lately Mom was on another planet.

The holidays were always a busy time for the bakery. They had to "make hay while the sun shines," as her dad had always said. This income had to last them through the lean months of January and February. This year, that extra income meant more. She had to catch up on their taxes. Did foreclosure lurk in their future?

She'd finished baking for the day. Turning off the ovens, she called Mrs. Wilcox. Might as well get this over with. Nathan's teacher was polite but firm. He'd called another boy a name and Sarah was shocked that he even knew that word. Jamie rarely swore.

"I know things are difficult right now," Mrs. Wilcox said, concern softening her voice.

"That's no excuse for bad behavior."

They agreed that Nathan would apologize. "This won't happen again," Sarah assured the teacher, feeling the weight of that promise.

Taking a deep breath, Sarah went out to check on her mother.

"Doesn't that case look wonderful?" Her mother greeted her. Sarah stood back from the counter, drinking in the orderly rows of pastries and cookies. Bread filled the racks along the wall behind the counter.

"It sure does. Ryan's a hard worker, but he burned his hands today."

"Oh, no. Poor boy."

"Mom, he's not a boy."

Her mother pursed her lips with one of her tick-a-lock expressions.

"He's got something on his mind. I don't know what." She studied the coffee machine. All the levers and buttons were intimidating. Mom was quiet and Sarah turned to find her staring out the front window in the direction of the library.

"Don't we all." Leaning over the display case, her mother propped her chin up with two hands.

"I said *something*, Mom. Not *someone*."

"What?" Her mom jerked. The woman was blissed out.

Nerves jumping, Sarah looked around. "Does it look bare in here?"

Her mom shrugged. "I suppose it's not very Christmasy."

"We need some decorations." One more thing on her list.

"The boxes are in the attic," her mother said, reaching for a white bakery box. "Guess I'll take some of these fresh cookies to the library. Stir up some business."

Suspicion set in. Sarah glanced out to the cold, empty street. "Is the library busy this time of year?"

Her mother hitched a shoulder. "Of course. Everyone wants to read their favorite Christmas story again."

Somehow Sarah doubted that. "I suppose the children's story hour brings a lot of young mothers." Mothers who didn't have time to bake.

A flush stained her mother's cheeks. "Actually, I've been asked to read to the children this coming Saturday." Her mother didn't look up as she filled a box with samples.

"Mom, you're taking our profits right out the door."

Lila stopped and Sarah felt terrible. She didn't want her mother worrying. "That's okay, Mom. Sorry."

But her mother quietly returned a couple of lemon bars to the tray.

"So tell me about the story hour. What will you read?"

"Frosty the Snowman. Rudolph. You know. The classics."

"I see." Stepping over to the coffee pot, Sarah decided it needed to be freshened. When she turned, she met her mother's eyes. How involved should she be with her mother's love life?

"What?" Mom lifted her brows, wrapping string around the box.

"Nothing." What was the use? Sarah held up the coffee carafe. "Guess I'll make a fresh pot." She sure would like to meet Stuart.

"How is Ryan working out in the back?" Her mother's question broke into Sarah's thoughts.

"He's doing fine." The words flew from her lips, maybe too quickly.

Her mother gave her a sly look. "I think he kind of likes you, Sarah."

"We need his help this holiday season."

"Oh, I think it's more than that." With a knowing smile and a girlish giggle, Mom got her coat from the back, swept up the cookies and headed to the library.

Sarah was left with questions.

Did Ryan like being around her? Or was it just family duty?

Seemed like he was pushing her to date. Did he want her to date him or other guys?

Sarah could drive herself crazy with questions like that. Bustling back to the work room, she glanced around with satisfaction. The bowls had been washed and dried. The baking sheets were criss-crossed neatly on the side board. Ryan had even set out the butter for the gingerbread cookies tomorrow. The cookie cutters sat ready.

If she were honest with herself, Sarah liked having him here. Her mother felt the same. She'd told Sarah that he reminded her of Jamie. He'd been the son Lila Wilkins never had and she'd taken his loss hard. And now it was the holidays. The time filled with memories of putting up a tree and decorating the house.

Sarah would have to make a point of including Ryan in any Christmas preparations. The boys would like that. Jamie would want her to make sure that everyone had a good holiday. He'd loved family get-togethers.

Marching back into the front, she flipped the coffee maker on, waiting until it gurgled and the smell of hazelnut filled the air. Who needed whipped cream on the top and all the other fancy stuff? But Ryan had a point and Daddy would agree. What could she do about it now?

Pent up energy made her jumpy. Taking the stairs two at a time, she found the tubs of Christmas decorations in the attic and lugged them down one by one. No matter what, she would make this holiday happy for everyone. That was a promise she'd made to herself and she intended to keep it.

When her mother got back from the library, she chattered endlessly about the cute Santa on the desk and how the "staff" were wearing reindeer horns with jingle bells. Sarah almost dropped the glittery red garland she was stringing along the counter.

That twinkle in her mother's eyes? Whatever was going on at the library was not about books.

# Chapter 7

Digging the key out from under the stiff, frozen mat, Ryan smiled. He should talk to her about this. Who else but Sarah would hide a key in such an obvious place? He opened the back door. Reaching inside, he snapped on the lights and the back room of the bakery came to life. Coming here in the early morning was a great way to start the day. The room was dark, silent and peaceful.

Ryan sniffed the air, still warm from yesterday's baking. In addition to sugar and yeasty dough, a faint whiff of Sarah's soap lingered. Smiling, he slipped off his coat. Even though he'd blasted the heat in his truck, he needed to warm up. Pushing through the swinging door, he entered the shop front. The feel of his boot adjustment was still new, and he enjoyed every step.

He snapped on the light. "Whoa." Sarah must have been busy. He hadn't glanced at the front when he came for his second shift. Christmas had exploded in the store with a blizzard of green and red. He blinked. On the main counter stood a red and gold Santa, settled into drifts of white fabric snow tucked with gold and red ornaments. Elves peeked from the shelves. In the center of each glass-topped table sat a small bowl of ornaments. Adhesive snowflakes dotted the plate glass window, as if there wasn't enough snow outside. The scent of pine tickled his nostrils. And he didn't miss the mistletoe handing from the light fixture.

Mistletoe and kissing. He couldn't even go there.

While the coffee perked, he studied the darkened street outside. Street lamps dropped pools of light on the snow. When he was growing up with Jamie, they loved the snow and cold. Despite their parents' warnings and threats, they'd take their sleds down to the ice floes banking the shoreline. Climbing to the top, they'd careen down the slick slopes, screaming with crazy fear.

Of course someone told their folks. The Pickard boys were at it again and were grounded for a month. Now Ryan wondered at the risks they'd taken back then. Grabbing his mug, he walked to the back.

For the next two hours he worked, punching the dough down, setting it to rise again. There was something satisfying about baking. Sure he loved the work on Harleys but it didn't bring the immediate satisfaction that The Full Cup did. He could understand now why his brother had fallen so easily into this role after Jamie married Sarah.

After the bread rose, he slid the sheets into the oven, his hand still tender from the burns. He became a mindless fool around Sarah. One look from her greenish blue eyes and he was toast.

By the time Sarah arrived, the racks were full of rye bread, sour dough, white and a multigrain twist he was trying out. He wondered how customers would like the prettier bread. Or maybe it was just another one of his stupid ideas.

Glancing around, Sarah's eyes brightened and he fed on that

light. "Ryan, I love to come in the morning and see this. You just don't know."

Ryan felt proud. Walking over, he took her coat.

"Such a gentleman," Sarah murmured, slipping her red scarf into the sleeve. "Thank you."

A bit disappointed that she still hadn't noticed anything different, he went to check on the cheese crowns. "Maybe today I won't burn these. Were there many complaints?"

"Oh, no. Not at all."

Ryan suspected that she wouldn't tell him even if people had missed the cheese crowns. "Today we're doing molasses cookies. You know —gingerbread men, Santas, Christmas trees and ornaments. That kind of thing."

"I noticed how you prettied up the place," Ryan said. She'd even put a bowl of holly on her desk.

"It's Christmas, doggone it." Sarah pushed up the sleeves of her red plaid shirt.

He swallowed a laugh. "You sound as if it's a chore."

Her lips twisted. "Isn't it? Sometimes you just have to put your life on remote."

"Sarah." But what could he say? He understood where she was this season.

With a sniff, she turned away. "Sorry, I'm feeling grouchy. The boys will have a good Christmas if it kills me."

"I'll help in any way I can."

"You're very sweet to us, Ryan." Her light touch on his arm ignited him. Then she turned. Bustling over to the one of oversize mixers, she banged a bowl into place and got to work.

Looking over the recipe, he could still feel the tingle of her touch. "Are you doubling or tripling in this recipe?"

"Tripling." Her grin was back and his shoulders eased. Her pain was hard to bear when he couldn't do anything about it.

"We need some music." She snapped on the radio and Bing Crosby was singing "White Christmas." "We'll have a white Christmas all right," she said.

"I like the snow." Looking out the back of the high windows, Ryan watched the snow shimmer under the alley light. "It reminds me, well, of stuff."

"Past Christmases?" A faint smile tilted her lips.

"Yeah. It's not bad to remember, is it?" He sure hoped not.

She shook her head slowly. "Our past is an important part of us. And we're making Christmas cookies. What could be better, right?"

"Right." But it wasn't going to be easy. Not for him. When the dough was made, the hard part started. The rolling pin Sarah was wielding? That sucker terrified him.

"Let's get to work." Grabbing a hunk of dough, Sarah sprinkled flour over the cutting board while Ryan's stomach knotted. Then she handed him the rolling pin. "Here you go. I'll frost the cheese crowns while you roll out the dough. Then choose your cookie cutters and have fun."

*Fun?* The lump in his throat felt big as that mound of dough.

First he swatted it down. Then he started to roll. Sweat broke out on his forehead as he pressed the rolling pin across the dough.

It would probably be bad to perspire on cookie dough. Sarah was humming along to the music but he wasn't having a "holly jolly Christmas." Not at all. He'd seen roadwork crews rolling out asphalt. Maybe that was the trick and he laid into it.

Meanwhile, he enjoyed watching Sarah frost the pastries. Her hands were so graceful, scooping up frosting and skimming the tops of the cheese crowns. How the heck did she do that?

"How's that molasses dough coming, Ryan?" Sarah asked, a twinkle in her eye, like she knew he was having a heck of a time.

He looked down. The dough was flattened so thin, he could see the table.

"Oh, my." Wiping the frosting from her hands, Sarah edged over, her lips twitching. "Um, I think we need a little more cookie than that, don't you?"

"I guess." Releasing the rolling pin, he ran his hands down his apron. They were throbbing from the pressure, not that he'd admit it.

"Let's give this another go." Gathering up the dough, Sarah worked some magic with her fingers. Suddenly he faced another mountainous mass. Ryan liked the lemon bars or brownies a lot better, where all you did was pour the batter into the pan.

"Don't look so disappointed." Reaching up, she pinched his chin gently between her fingers. "Everyone has to learn."

She was so close that he could see the pulse throbbing at the base of her throat. Then she dropped her gaze and swallowed. "Guess we should get to work."

"Right." Gripping the rolling pin so hard that his hands hurt, he nodded. "Yep, Let's get on with it." He attacked the mound of dough.

"Oh, Ryan," she murmured. "Softer. You're not trying to kill the cookie dough."

"Okay, boss lady." How could she be so patient with him? The one time his mother did try to make cookies the whole mess ended in the trash can and Mom took off for the bakery.

Now he *was* the bakery—or acting like it. He had to get this right so Sarah wasn't embarrassed by his cookies.

"Here let me help." Her arms went around him and Ryan froze. Suddenly they were rolling cookie dough together, her hands on his. He'd never felt anything so sexy in his life.

"Can you feel it?" she asked. "Just roll softly, softly."

"Yep, I sure can," he croaked out. He wouldn't think about the warm breath on his neck. The vibration of her voice against his back. When the dough became a perfect circle, he figured it was a miracle.

But it wasn't the cookie dough he wanted. No, he wanted to turn and take her in his arms. Kiss her sweet lips until they had to come up for air.

She was driving him crazy.

*Jamie I told you I'd always watch out for Sarah. That's all I'm trying to do.*

But that was a lie. And he never could lie to his brother.

Sarah kept moving behind him, angling her head so she could see. "Just a little bit here and a little bit there."

A lot could happen as a result of that little bit. When her body moved, every pore in his body leapt to life. Was he sweating bullets? Sure felt like it.

This could get embarrassing.

Then she released his hands and stepped back. Fresh air passed between them. "How's that?" She blinked up at him in that innocent way she had.

"Fine. Just fine." Irritation roughened his voice. He felt like diving into one of the snow banks. Maybe for her this was just another lesson.

She backed away. He took a breath.

"Well then." Her eyes skittered from the ovens to the clock— anywhere but him. "Grease the baking sheet and choose your cookie cutters.'

"Sure. Right."

"I'll just get back..." Her arm hand waved and her mouth opened. But nothing came out. Maybe she wasn't so calm after all.

"Back to work, boss lady." There. That sounded authoritative. But he was putty—or cookie dough—in her hands.

So he started with the cookie cutters. Before she even finished her frosting work, he had three pans filled with gingerbread boys, reindeer and fat Santas.

Footsteps sounded on the back stairs just as he took the last pan from the oven. "Well don't you two look busy." Mrs. Wilkins stood there in a pretty pink sweater.

"Hi, Mom." Walking over, Sarah kissed her mother's cheek. She was like that. Dropping kisses as she went.

"We're working on molasses cookies," he said. The spicy smell filled the room.

"So I see." She glanced over at the table littered with cookie cutters.

"I'm going to clean those," he murmured.

Sarah's mother tied on her apron. "How's your Christmas season going, Ryan?"

"Just fine." This was probably the best Christmas he'd ever had.

She smiled with the same wise eyes her daughter had inherited. "Thanks for taking my place back here."

"No problem. I enjoy working in the bakery."

"Your brother did too." Picking up a piece of leftover cookie dough, Lila rolled it in her fingers. Then she formed an S with the dough. "Sarah, remember how we used to make our initials with the leftovers?"

"Sure do." A small smile on her lips, Sarah started playing with the leftover dough. Then she dropped it and turned. "Guess we should frost them now."

Her mother left and Sarah filled two tubes with the white frosting. If the rolling pin struck fear into his heart, that was nothing compared to that plump tube in his hand. Of course for Sarah, it was child's play. A little squirt here and another one there and Santa looked great, decorated with white.

He tried. Really he did. But he pressed too hard and blobs of frosting shot out, not the delicate lines and swirls on Sarah's pieces.

He tried again. Ah, better.

But not for Sarah. "Hmm. Let's count that as a trial piece."

What? Okay, so the cookie looked a little blobby. It would taste the same. But he did it again.

"Better." Sarah was peering over his shoulder. He couldn't resist. Turning, he squirted her. First she looked shocked. Then she got mad.

"So that's how you want to play it." Frosting dripped from her forehead onto her cheek. Her tongue darted out. Grabbing another pastry tube, she took aim and hit him right between the eyes.

"Game on." Chasing her around the butcher block table, he went nuts. This was like paint ball but even better. And Sarah gave as good as she got.

"Take that," she'd yell.

"Oh, really? How about this?"

Frosting was flying and their faces were covered by the time by the bags were empty. Shoulder to shoulder, they collapsed against the counter, laughing until they were breathless. It had been so long since he'd heard Sarah laugh. Her mother peeked over the door and then faded away.

~.~

Messy with frosting, Ryan looked adorable. Adorable and hunky. Standing there babbling, Sarah felt like a fool. The man did have a way about him. How had she ever missed that? Gone was Jamie's irritating little brother. That old image didn't fit anymore.

He'd made her laugh. And it felt good.

Her heart beat in time to "Little Saint Nick," blasting from the radio. Why had she wrapped her arms around him like that? Hadn't once been enough the other day? Maybe that was the problem. She knew how Ryan's broad shoulders tapering down to a slim waist felt and, mercy, she liked it. He'd been so darn cute working with that frosting, biting his lower lip in concentration.

Checking the clock, he laid the bag down. "Okay, if I leave, boss lady?" He gave her one of his mischievous grins. "There's a Harley waiting for me up at Branson's."

"Sure. No problem."

Taking off the apron, he folded it into a neat square and then hesitated. "Maybe I'll just take this home and wash it. It's a mess."

"You'll do no such thing." She took it from his hands. "I'll just throw it in with mine."

Funny but she liked the idea of their laundry twining together in the washer.

"Okay. Thanks, Sarah." Dashing over to the sink, Ryan washed his hands. His apron in her hands, she felt dazed, like the time Mildred Wentworth had accidentally side-swiped Sarah's car in the parking lot at Clancy's.

Turning, he dried his hands on a towel. "Don't you notice anything different about me?"

Sarah's head jerked and her eyes focused. "What?"

Slipping the towel on the toolbar, he grunted. "Never mind." Shaking his head, he mumbled something she couldn't understand. When he pulled on his huge sheepskin coat, she thought of what Chili had said about macho man. Maybe she was right. In that coat, Ryan should be out on the plains herding cattle. The image sent a warm rush through her.

"See you later," he said, ducking out the door.

"Later." The room seemed to deflate after he left.

Ryan must be exhausted, holding down his job at Branson's and driving here to help out. How she wished she could pay him. But having another person on the payroll would be stretching it. Eager to get the cute cookies into the case, she arranged them on a fresh tray and carried it to the front. Her mother was ringing up a sale so she slipped behind her. The customers left. "More people from the library," she said with a sassy smile.

"That's good, Mom." Going around to the front, Sarah checked the cookie display and smiled, remembering what fun she'd had with Ryan that morning.

"Are you going to bring the boys to hear me read Christmas stories this Saturday?"

"Sure. Of course." How would she cover the shop? "I'll work something out."

Humming to herself, her mother spritzed the counter tops and wiped them down with paper towels. But her eyes were dreamy as she worked. Mom had always been a very practical, no nonsense woman. Sarah might have to tell her to ease up on the purple eye shadow but didn't have the heart. She seemed so happy.

Going into the back, Sarah called Lindsay.

"What's up?" Lindsay said when she picked up. "Haven't seen you much lately."

"Busy baking Christmas cookies. It's kind of my last hurrah before people take off for the winter break."

"Break? Tanner and I are staying right here."

"Uh, huh." Sarah pictured the two of them cuddled and cozy in

Tanner's home above the dunes with her two girls, Rebecca and Susan. Although she was happy for her friend, her heart twisted a bit. "I'm calling to ask a favor."

"Name it," Lindsay said with no hesitation.

"My mother is reading for the Children's Hour at the library this Saturday. Could you watch the shop for maybe an hour or so?"

"No problem, even though this is like letting the fox into the chicken coop. All that pastry to sample while you're gone."

Lindsay was thin as a strand of dune grass. "I'm trusting you. A new librarian has taken Mildred Wentworth's place. My mother's acting weird so I have to check him out."

She could hear her friend release her breath. "Your mother is dating?"

*Dating. Mom?* Reaching over, she picked a letter she'd baked from the leftover dough. Biting down, she munched for a moment.

"Sarah, are you still there?"

She swallowed. "Yes, sorry. Just thinking. I want to meet Stuart. You know, casually."

"Stuart. Hmm. A very distinguished name."

"You think so?" She took another bite.

"What are you eating?" Lindsay asked.

Sarah glanced down at the half eaten letter. "Oh, no. I've eaten Ryan."

"What?" Lindsay howled.

Heat flooded Sarah's face. "A cookie. I just ate the R."

"See you Saturday." Lindsay was chortling as Sarah hung up.

## Chapter 8

"Can I help you?" Standing behind the desk of the Gull Harbor library, Stuart Martin was tall and slender with the kindest eyes Sarah had ever seen. No wonder her mother brought him cookies.

"Mom, come on!" Nathan and Justin pulled at her hands. They'd been restless since she got them home Friday.

"I've come to hear my mother read to the children today."

A smile creased Stuart's face and made his blue eyes sparkle behind the Buddy Holly glasses. "Of course. I suspect you know where she is." He waved toward the back. In his houndstooth jacket and blue shirt he cut quite the figure.

The hum of voices echoed from the children's nook, and she wanted the boys to get a seat. "Thank you." Sarah led Nathan and Justin past the stacks of books and computer stations into the children's area.

Holding a large book with Frosty on the cover, Mom gave her a nod. "We'll wait until our newcomers get seated." On the floor around Mom were sprawled at least a dozen children, their snow jackets piled on one of the low desks. The small room smelled like wet snowsuits. Mothers sat cramped in the small chairs, looking as if Christmas was catching up to them.

When Nathan suddenly stopped, Sarah nearly stumbled over him. Had he gotten stubborn again? When she served him a hot dog last night, he'd refused. But when her mother gave Nathan a stern look, he sank down, unzipped this jacket and handed it to Sarah. Justin was already settled, legs crossed and eyes on the book.

The Children's Story Hour would be her Saturday break. For at least thirty minutes she wasn't responsible for her children's well-being—a relief to any mother. Besides, she enjoyed listening to *Frosty the Snowman*. Sarah scanned the room. During the holidays parents seemed to develop dark circles under their eyes, deep yawns and, yes, sometimes colds. Quite a few sniffles and even some coughs went around the room. Mom began to read.

As her mother showed the children the pictures, the overhead lights made her blonde hair look like a halo. She looked so pretty in her fluffy pink sweater, green ornament earrings bobbing from her ears.

Surrendering to the soothing cadence of her mother's voice, Sarah closed her eyes. The hum of the heating system helped her doze off. In her dreams she wasn't thinking of her little boys. Oh no. She was under the mistletoe she'd hung up at work, looking into eyes as warm as brownies just taken from the oven. When Ryan bent for a kiss, her pulse kicked up. Almost there. She was almost there.

Applause ruptured her dream. Sarah blinked and straightened. Her cheek felt damp and she swiped at a trail of telltale drool. No one was looking at her, though. Joining the clapping, she felt happy for her mom, who was clutching the closed book to her chest and blushing. No one seemed to appreciate the presentation more than Stuart Martin, standing in the doorway.

Well, well. Whatever magic the library had worked, Sarah was grateful. Her mother worked so hard. The bakery and her boys seemed to be Mom's whole life. Didn't she deserve more? While the other mothers struggled with coats and mittens, Sarah worked her way through to her mother. The boys reached Mom first.

"You did great, Grandma." Justin hugged his grandmother's legs.

"Thank you, dear." She patted his head.

"Yeah," Nathan said. "We're going to make a snowman just like Frosty this Christmas. Right, Justin?"

"You bet!" Justin's eyes gleamed in anticipation.

"Who is going to help you create this snowy wonder?" Sarah teased, expecting them to name her.

"Uncle Ryan!" both boys said in chorus.

Mom exchanged a look with Stuart and then smiled at Sarah.

Well. What was that about?

"Can we go home now?" Nathan nudged her.

"But I want some books." Justin folded his arms across his chest. "When we come to the library, we always take home books."

Yes, they did. The other mothers held books. They'd probably gotten here early, more organized than Sarah. "Fine. You can each choose three."

Pleased, Justin scampered off and Nathan followed, still grumbling.

Sarah headed straight for her mother and Stuart, now engaged in deep conversation.

"Wasn't your mother wonderful?" he asked as Sarah approached.

"You did great." Her mom's face flushed when Sarah hugged her. "I've heard that story a million times. You made it sound new."

Her mother threw her a wry look. "Sarah, thank you. But you fell asleep after the first page. I completely understand. It's been a long week."

"We really appreciate the cookies you send over." But Stuart was thinking of more than gingerbread and lemon bars as he smiled at her mother. "Our patrons love them."

"Mom's become a great marketer." Sarah dove right into it. "Where do you call home, Stuart?"

"Syracuse, New York, where the winters are as cold as they are here."

They all laughed. "How did Mildred ever find you?" Sarah continued.

"Through an ad in a magazine for librarians. Christmas at Gull Harbor seemed just like the change I needed." A shadow fell over his eyes.

She should have stopped there. "Why is that?"

"This would be my first Christmas alone. I just thought something different..." His voice trailed off.

"I see." What a dear man. "We're glad you came to Gull Harbor."

He brightened. "I am too. Imagine meeting your mother who

enjoys ancient civilizations as much as I do."

Sarah couldn't even look at her mom.

"And she brings me cookies." He had the cutest way of saying that word with a hard k, glancing at her mom as he said it.

"For people visiting the library," her mother reminded him.

"Well, of course." Stuart would probably agree with anything her mother said.

"And after Mildred gets back?" She didn't want to see her mother hurt when Stuart returned to Syracuse.

"Stuart lives in the moment," her mother said, hugging the book she'd just read as if she wished her arms were around something—or someone—else.

"Well, Lindsay is watching the store. I should get back." If she expected her mother to offer to tend the store, she was mistaken. Smiling up at the tall librarian, Mom was totally googly-eyed.

Stuart extended his hand. "So nice to meet you, Sarah. Your mother has said such wonderful things about you. Could I ask you a question?"

"Of course." The boys were stacking books onto one of the tables.

"I'm just curious. Why is your store called The Full Cup when it seems like more of a bakery? All those wonderful cookies come my way but no coffee."

"Oh, Stu, you don't need all that caffeine." Mom playfully squeezed his arm.

*Stu?* This was more serious than Sarah realized. Once again Sarah ended up telling a man the background of the coffee shop that turned into a bakery. No one in Gull Harbor seemed to find that strange, but then they knew the history. Lila had a problem with all those levers.

Obviously, Stuart had never heard that story. "Couldn't you maximize your revenues by offering the espresso drinks other stores sell?"

Okay, so Stuart knew corporate talk.

"Of course. But we're very busy." She wasn't going to admit that her mother, the woman who had somehow become an expert in ancient cultures, couldn't work the coffee machine. "My brother-in-law was just asking the same question this week."

Mom tore her attention from Stuart. "Ryan asked you about the coffee?"

"Yes, he did." Worse things could happen to her mother than Stuart Martin, Sarah decided. "Maybe you could come for dinner sometime, Stuart."

"I'd be delighted." He beamed at Mom as if he'd just been offered a year of free pastries.

While Justin stood quietly waiting with his books, Nathan was glowering at her. Still, Sarah had questions. "Could I ask why you are so interested in coffee?"

Stuart sucked in a breath. "I'm afraid my family is very involved in the coffee trade." Almost embarrassed, he named a nationally know franchise. On anyone else, she may have considered this name dropping. But with Stuart, it seemed cute. His reddened cheeks helped.

"They weren't very understanding when I decided to become a

librarian," Stuart said. "But here I am. Semi-retired. This temporary position seemed perfect for me."

"I hope to see you soon." While she absorbed that information, Sarah clapped her hands to get the boys' attention. Stuart hurried back to the front desk and her mother helped Sarah zip Nathan and Justin into their jackets.

Sarah had gathered so much information that her head was whirling.

Ryan tossed the wrench on the floor. The sound of metal hitting concrete echoed in the large garage and the other guys looked over. "Hey, keep it down!" Manuel called out.

"Right." The radio was blasting. The men were telling jokes while they worked and he was in a foul mood. Repairing this Harley cam chain had turned into a real pain. Usually, he enjoyed the challenge. Not today.

Today he was trying to forget the bluish green eyes of the woman who'd hugged him while he was making cookies. Well, *trying* to make cookies. That frosting fight had been something else and he smiled. Leaning back on his elbows, he tried to remember how soft Sarah had felt against him when they rolled out the blasted cookie dough together.

A foot nudged his boot. "You taking a nap or what?" Stanley asked.

"Just got something in my eye." And he jammed a knuckle in his right eye. "This cam chain is giving me trouble."

Stanley lifted a bushy eyebrow. "The guy who could take apart a Harley with his eyes closed is having trouble?"

Giving a gritty groan, Ryan sat up. "You got that right."

"Come into the office and take a load off." Stanley led the way. "You were working when I got here. It's past lunchtime."

Since Ryan didn't help out at The Full Cup on Saturdays, he was trying to put in a lot of hours at Branson's. "I could use a cup of coffee." Ryan could use a lot of stuff but nothing he could mention to Stanley.

Inside the glass-enclosed office, the noise level dropped. "So what's your son doing today?" Ryan asked.

Pouring a mug of coffee that sure smelled good, Stanley smiled. "Phoebe's got him putting up their Christmas tree."

Putting up the tree. It had been a long time since Ryan had done that. Memories rolled over him. The smell of pine and the sticky feeling of sap on your fingers. Working through knotted tree lights, only to find that they'd burned out. All things that used to irritate him now taunted him with their absence.

Ryan took the full mug Stanley offered and topped it off with cream and sugar. "She didn't even notice."

Stanley lowered himself into the worn chair that rocked back to just the right angle. "She didn't notice what?" But the older man's eyes went to Ryan's boots.

"The way I walk now." He extended a leg. "Not a word about it."

After blowing on his coffee, Stanley took a sip and smacked his lips. "Get over yourself. You got to understand, Ryan. All women are different." The old chair squeaked when Stanley rocked it.

"That's real profound, Stanley." Ryan enjoyed teasing the old man and took another sip of coffee.

"Not that I'm an expert or anything because I certainly am not."

"You helped get Ryder and Phoebe back together. That's saying something." Ryder had been angrier than a wet cat in winter the whole year after his divorce from Phoebe Hunicutt until his dad stepped in. "Phoebe adores you."

"Let's just say it's mutual." Stanley wore a pleased smile. "I'm looking forward to Christmas dinner with them. Last year was the pits."

"What hints did you give him for marital bliss?" Ryan was only half kidding.

Stanley got grumbly. "I'm not a man who hints at anything. You young guys sometimes have rocks for brains."

"Thanks, Stanley, I needed that." But Ryan wasn't offended. After all, Stanley was the one who had a place to go on holidays. Sarah hadn't mentioned anything yet about Christmas dinner.

Twiddling his thumbs, Stanley studied the overhead light. "I told him to hang in there. To put himself right in front that girl's face. You know Ryder had his pride. Sure, you're there, baking and whatever. But are you showing her how important you could be in her life?"

Ryan didn't know what to make of that. "I'm working part time there. And then I barrel up here to work, not that I'm complaining. What else can I do?"

Stanley pressed a hand to his chest. "You poor thing. My heart pumps peanut butter for you. You all tired out?"

Absolutely no sympathy in the old man's voice. Ryan took another gulp of coffee. "In some ways, yeah. Not in others."

The two men shared a look. Enough said. Stanley went back to twirling his thumbs and Ryan went back to wishing. Time to put all the cards on the table. "I don't know if Sarah thinks of me as anything but her brother-in-law. Maybe she's just being nice to me."

"What do you mean? She must want you around or you wouldn't be there."

Ryan ran a hand through hair that needed a trim bad. "Sarah's always belonged to Jamie. She's sweet and nice and..."

"And what?" Stanley looked puzzled.

"Did you just move here?" Not one for words, Ryan was sputtering. He knew Stanley was older than water and had been here all his life.

The chair creaked when the old man leaned forward. "Where we've been isn't where we're going. Everybody makes mistakes. If my own sweet Marietta was still here, she'd tell you all about mine. Sarah isn't pushing you away, is she?"

"Not that I noticed." He squeezed his eyes tight, thinking of Sarah's arms around him, helping roll the darn dough.

When he opened them, Stanley was beaming. "Now son, it's Christmas time. There's a lot of stuff that has to be done. What is Ryder doing today? When Phoebe gets home from her hair salon, he'll have the tree up and the lights will be on. At least that's what he told me. You do something nice for a lady and she notices. You can't just tell her. You have to show her."

But Sarah wasn't Phoebe and Ryan sure as heck wasn't Ryder. "I see her every day, practically. After all, I work for her."

That earned a finger wag. "And that's the point, isn't it? Try to get outside the bakery. Include those little boys of hers."

"I've always done anything she asked. School programs. Mowing the lawn when she hurt her back."

"But she had to ask you?" The beetle brows peaked.

"I didn't want to bother her, okay?" The words came out as fast as the mental images zipping through his mind. "Maybe I've been doing this all wrong. I did clean the snow off her car once."

"Once?"

"Yeah." He thought back. "Maybe more than once."

Stanley grinned. "That's a good start, son. But you've got a ways to go."

## Chapter 9

"Stamp the snow off your boots, boys." Sarah struggled to open the front door of the coffee shop. The wind wasn't cooperating. One strong push and they fell into the warm, cinnamon scented air. She'd scattered a bag of fragrant pinecones around the shop. Her Christmas decorations really did perk up the store. But Sarah's Christmas spirit still hadn't arrived.

Paper towel in hand, Lindsay was spritzing the display counter.

"Do you have to clean wherever you go?" Sarah teased.

With a playful shrug, her friend tucked their cleaning supplies under the register. "It's a habit. That's what I do—clean people's cottages."

"How was the story hour, boys?" Lindsay had two little girls, and she always made a fuss over Nathan and Justin."

"Grandma was great," Justin said. "I love Frosty. We're going to make a snow man just like him."

Nathan didn't look as enthusiastic as his little brother. "Yeah, it was fine."

Sarah helped the boys off with their jackets. "Was it very busy here?"

"I could handle it. What would you like today, boys?" Lindsay looked like a natural behind that counter. "We have fresh gingerbread boys with frosting."

"I want one! I want a gingerbread boy." Justin pressed his nose against the glass.

"So much for my cleaning." Lindsay chuckled.

Sarah gave herself a shake. She couldn't wander around in a tired daze all holiday season. "One cookie, boys. Then off you to go to color. Hear me?"

Nathan turned away. "I don't want a cookie."

Sarah bit her tongue and prayed for patience. "Then you can go back and color."

"Coloring's for babies." With that he swatted through the swinging door so hard, it hit the doorframe. Sarah counted to ten.

Justin pointed to his choice and Lindsay whipped out the gingerbread man. Then he disappeared after his brother. With a sigh, Sarah took off her coat and piled it on top of theirs. "I need coffee." Sarah headed for the pot in the corner and Lindsay joined her at a window table. Frost had etched the window with an icy pattern.

"Marriage agrees with you." Sitting down at a table, Sarah nudged a full cup toward Lindsay and then filled her own mug with sugar and cream.

"I've only been married about a month, but yes, I'm happy," Lindsay said with a sigh of contentment. Sarah felt a twinge of jealousy, followed by guilt. After all, Lindsay was a good friend.

"Tanner makes you happy?"

Her lips tipping into a smile, Lindsay nodded. "I never thought

I'd say this but yes. Of course I have my girls too. But you know how that goes. Rebecca and Susan are little and they..."

"...can be a pain sometimes," Sarah said. "A responsibility. Not that I'm complaining."

"How is your holiday going?" Lindsay's forehead wrinkled into friendly concern.

"I'm behind as usual. Ryan's agreed to work some hours here. Mom's getting older so she minds the store. That back room with heavy trays and heat might not be the place for her anymore."

"She is getting on," Lindsay agreed.

Smiling, Sarah thought about Lila and the librarian. "She's mighty spry when she wants to be."

Lindsay leaned closer. "How was the librarian?"

"Oh, Stuart is quite an eyeful if you're over sixty."

Lindsay's eyes brightened. "Wow. Good for her."

Smiling to herself, Sarah took another sip. "My mother takes cookie samples to the library almost every day."

"Has it helped business?"

"Yes." Sarah chuckled. "Have you seen my mother lately?"

"No, I've been so busy. Our rentals went from football games to cross country skiing, not that I'm complaining." In addition to cleaning cottages, she also had a rental service with Mercedes.

"My mother is now blonde."

Lindsay snorted on the coffee.

Getting up, Sarah grabbed more napkins and handed them to her sputtering friend. "Are you okay?"

"Yes." Blotting the tears from her eyes, Lindsay sucked in some air. "Give me a warning before you lay that kind of news on me, okay?"

"She noticed your mother's hair at your wedding. But I do think meeting Stuart gave her that extra little push."

Lindsay's mouth fell open. "That's amazing. How does she look?"

"Ten years younger and she acts like it too."

"I say, go for it." Lifting her mug, Lindsay took a sip. "What about you, Sarah? Have you ever thought of going out with someone?"

"Oh, no." The acid from the coffee gnawed at her stomach. "Haven't got time. Where would I find a man anyway?"

"We talked about this last summer, Sarah. Then Tanner came into my life."

Reaching over, she squeezed Lindsay's hand. "I'm so happy that happened for you, Lindsay. Really I am. But how many single men are there in Gull Harbor?"

"What about Ryan?"

She stared at her friend blankly. "What about him?"

"The times I've seen you together at school events? I've always thought your brother-in-law had a secret thing for you. Well, since, you know, Jamie."

"Oh, I don't know." Sarah twisted a curl at the nape of her neck.

"Sometimes we can't see what's right in front of us. Or we don't want to see," Lindsay added quietly.

The conversation had turned totally crazy. Sarah pushed her

mug aside. She'd had enough coffee for today. From the back room came the sound of the boys arguing.

Checking her watch, Lindsay got up. "Never overlook the man closest to your heart."

Sarah stood and gathered the napkins and mugs. "What the heck does that mean?"

Lindsay lifted a brow. "When you're making those cookies with Ryan, maybe you should take a good look at him. He's a hunk. Sure, he was little crazy when he was younger but hasn't that changed?"

"He's very...responsible." *Hot. Sweet. Thoughtful.*

"Responsible?" The way Lindsay tossed that out, you'd think it had become a bad word. "You sound like his mother."

The comment reminded her of Ryan's painful history. "His mother ditched them, you know. Poor boy, his parents took a one way ticket to Chicago. They eventually divorced and his mom remarried. Ryan rarely mentions her."

"How can a woman do that?" Lindsay said as they pushed through the swinging doors. The boys were arguing about something. Justin was on the brink of tears.

"Nathan started it," Justin whined.

"Did not."

"Nathan." Sarah fisted her hands on her hips.

"Sure reminds me of my girls," Lindsay said in an undertone. "I should get going. My mother has them today, not that Mom and Dad mind. They're headed to Florida after the holidays."

"Sounds nice." Her mother would probably love a vacation like that. She deserved one.

After Lindsay left, Sarah gave the boys a Santa puzzle she'd been saving for a moment like this. Even Nathan looked pleased. With the bell jingled in the shop, she hurried back to the front. A young family was picking out cookies and pastries. "Guests for dinner," the young mother said. Chatting away, Sarah filled a bakery box. Their stock was getting low. Maybe she should make up a list of what she wanted to bake with Ryan this week.

The family left and Sarah wandered to the front window. Touching one hand to the glass, she watched the family drive away. Lucky family.

When the phone rang, she almost didn't answer. Maybe it was her mother. She took the phone from her pocket.

"Hey, it's me. Ryan."

"Hey." Warmth spilled through her.

"What are you and the boys doing tomorrow afternoon?"

"Nothing much." So many chores waited for her at home. Decorate the house. Put up the artificial tree she'd bought with Jamie five years ago.

"*The Grinch That Stole Christmas* is playing at the old theater in South Haven. Would you and boys like to see it with me?" His voice wavered a bit as if he were uncertain.

By that time, Sarah had pushed through the door to the back. The boys were huddled over the puzzle. They'd made progress on Santa's head and one of the reindeer. "Uncle Ryan wants to know if you'd like to see the Grinch movie tomorrow. You guys aren't interested, right?"

Nathan jumped up so fast he knocked over the chair. "I want to go."

"Me too," Justin said. "You're coming right, Mommy?"

With a smile she went back to the phone. "I think that's a yes."

The boys had both settled back, heads almost touching over the puzzle. Looked like they were having a private conversation. Lately, they'd been so secretive.

Ryan's laugh rippled over the phone and right up her spine. "Great. See you tomorrow then." They set a time.

"You bet." Ending the call, Sarah felt hungry. The gingerbread men were calling. Returning to the sunny front room, she grabbed a cookie and crunched down. Remembering their frosting fight brought on a fit of giggles.

She could hardly wait for tomorrow.

At least the roads weren't bad as Ryan drove Sarah and the boys up to South Haven on Sunday. So far this year people were happy to see the snow. The white stuff was "Christmasy." Usually those were the women who didn't have to drive in it. Stanley and the other guys in Branson Motors laughed about it all winter. The garage did a lot of plowing, and Ryder earned extra cash. Today the roads were salted and the blue stuff glittered in the sunlight.

Sitting next to him, Sarah looked amazing in a dark green coat and her red scarf. She smelled good too. Snow had caught in her hair and was slowly melting. Getting out of the shop was probably good for her. But the boys were suspiciously quiet in the back.

Glancing in the rearview mirror, Ryan saw they had their eyes trained on the front seat. "What's up with you two today? Cat got your tongues?"

"We don't have a cat," Justin said very seriously.

"Ryan was kidding," Nathan said with the tone of an older brother who thought he knew it all.

"Maybe we need some music." Leaning over she fiddled with a knob on the dashboard. But she didn't know the stations.

Reaching for the buttons, he brushed her hand. She didn't back away. Using all the restraint he could muster, Ryan gently set her soft hand back in her lap. He wanted to cup it under his own, but she'd be horrified. "Getting reception can be tricky up here. I have the buttons set." He punched them until Christmas music filled the truck.

"I'll never get tired of 'Silent Night,' " she said wistfully.

"Probably because you don't have one, not with these two clowns." He glanced in the mirror. "And that means you two."

"Hey, we're being good." Nathan seemed to give his younger brother a signal.

"Yep, we are," Justin said. "I'm not even kicking the back of your seat with my boots."

Ryan laughed. "Well, good." No wonder Sarah looked so tired sometimes. Keeping up with these two was work.

When the music switched to "We Wish You A Merry Christmas," Sarah leaned closer. "I met Mom's librarian yesterday."

"What did you think?"

"I liked him. He's tall and attractive in a studious kind of way.

And he seems to have a thing for my mom, that's for sure."

"Glad to hear it." He really liked Lila Wilkins.

"Hey, what are you two talking about up there?" Nathan leaned forward until the seatbelt caught him.

"Why don't you and Justin count the signs along the road?" Ryan used to play that game with Jamie on road trips. "Justin, you count yellow signs and Nathan will count the white ones."

"Do we get a prize?" Justin asked. Ryan should have seen that coming.

"Sure." He caught Sarah's eyes and they smiled at each other.

"What's the prize going to be?" Always one for details, Nathan drilled down.

"Don't pester your uncle like that. Just play the game, okay?" Sarah looked flustered, as if she thought the boys were bothering him. They weren't. He liked having the little guys around. It was like having a piece of his brother back. He pressed one boot to the accelerator. Yeah, it felt fine. He'd tested it after he picked up his boot.

The truck became peaceful except for the boys counting. When they reached the theater, he quickly found a parking spot on the street.

"I always like this old theater," Sarah said as they helped the boys from the truck. "Reminds me of when I was a kid. My folks would bring me up here."

"Me too. The yellow bricks and the old red sign are from another time or place. I'm glad they didn't tear it down, the way some towns have."

They hurried across the street. Although Sarah protested, Ryan paid for the tickets. The warm smell of fresh popcorn filled the air and bright red signage lured them to the refreshment counter. "You two boys don't like popcorn, do you?"

Well, that caused a row. Sarah insisted that they share two bags and wanted to pay, but Ryan wasn't having that. He worked hard and saved well—a secret his brother had taught him. "Save so you can spend on what you really want." And this? He liked the feeling of walking down the aisle with Sarah and the boys. The theater was about half full, mostly with families.

"Let's put the boys between us," Sarah said when they came to an empty row.

"No," Nathan said with that stubborn tilt to his chin. "You and Uncle Ryan sit in the middle. Right, Justin?" He looked to his brother for agreement.

"Right. I'll sit next to Mom."

The theater lights dimmed. "Enough." Ryan nudged Nathan's shoulder. They hustled into their seats.

During the previews, Ryan caught Nathan looking around them to catch Justin's eye. Yeah, something was brewing. Were they playing matchmaker? It just felt good to be sitting here, passing the popcorn back and forth while they sipped sodas and laughed.

What would this Christmas be like if he didn't have Sarah and the kids? Once his mother had suggested that he consider moving to Chicago. "Get out of that podunk town," was how she put it.

But what would he do in Chicago? Besides, he liked this podunk town. His mother had no time to be a grandmother. That had always been clear to Jamie. Usually she sent the boys a check for their birthdays. Ryan loved spending time with them.

As the Grinch schemed up on the screen, Ryan felt he was sitting just where he should be. Next to him, Sarah chuckled and ate popcorn. The seats felt small and he was tempted to stretch an arm around her shoulders. But she might freak out.

So he sat in silence, watching the screen, but not seeing it. Instead, his mind replayed rolling out the cookie dough with Sarah's arms around him. He smiled, remembering squirting her with frosting.

All too soon the movie ended and the lights came on. Helping the kids on with their coats and gathering the trash, he felt every bit like a father. Sure, he wished Jamie could be here, enjoying his sons. But sometimes life took a turn you never figured on. What else could you do but deal with it? Ryan squared his shoulders.

But Sarah was more than a duty. Much more.

As he moved up the aisle, he let one hand fall on her shoulder. She fell back a bit as if for comfort, her soft curls brushing his chin. Very softly, he kissed the top of her head. She never even felt it.

Outside, it was getting dark. Sarah waved to some friends. Lindsay and Tanner had just gotten married. "Well, look who's here." She gave Lindsay a big hug. Two little girls were with them and from what he remembered, the kids belong to Lindsay.

Sarah introduced him to Tanner and then kept babbling with her girlfriend. "So what's next on your Sunday agenda?"

"We're going home to decorate our tree," Lindsay said. "Gotta run." With a wave, the four of them broke off. Ryan, Sarah and the boys continued down the snowy street.

"Have you put up your tree?" he asked when they got to the truck. Ryan opened the back door and the boys climbed inside.

"No, I haven't gotten our artificial tree up yet," she whispered to him. "I still have to put it together."

"A fake tree?" He was falling down on the job. "Well then, I guess next week we should get one. I know a guy with woods thick with real trees. You can't celebrate Christmas without a tree, can you?"

"That's wonderful, Ryan, if it's no trouble." She blinked up at him, her eyes turning green as any pine sprig.

"Trust me. You are no trouble." Their eyes caught and held.

Then she dipped her head and climbed in. Unspoken words danced through his head as he circled to the other side.

Pulling away from the curb, Ryan thought he heard Nathan say to his brother, "See. It's working."

~.~

The day had been special. The boys looked so happy as she helped them with their prayers and got them settled. That contentment carried her to bed.

"Oh, Jamie," she said that night, his picture in her hand. "I know you'd want our boys to have days like today. This is just what you would do. And you'd be proud of Ryan. He's turned into such a good man."

But she couldn't share everything that was in her heart.

## Chapter 10

The smell of pine hung rich and heavy in the air as they trudged
through the woods, looking for the perfect Christmas tree. The
only sound was the soft thud of snow shaken free by the breeze.
Sarah yanked her red scarf higher around her ears. Ryan walked
ahead with the boys, chainsaw hanging from a strap around his
shoulder. She enjoyed looking at the three of them.

"See anything you like, boys?" she asked.

Bundled into their jackets, only their faces were visible. Against
Nathan's protests, she'd made them both wear snowpants today.

"Not yet," Nathan said very seriously. You'd think they were
shopping for a car, not a tree. The idea of having a fresh tree this
year had excited the boys. She pictured one a little taller than she
was with thick heavy branches. In the attic were boxes of family
ornaments.

"The trees are so big." Justin's voice was filled with awe. Sarah
totally understood. Most of the pines towered above them. She
didn't know how they'd ever drag one of these out of the woods
owned by Stanley Branson, Phoebe's father-in-law.

Turning, Ryan smiled. Cheeks red from the cold, he was in his
element out here. Snowflakes dotted the mane of hair that wouldn't

be contained by his green cap. "You look like Paul Bunyan," she teased. "A mountain man."

"Do I?" He shifted his shoulders, as if he liked the compliment. "What kind of tree do you have in mind, guys?"

"We don't know yet." Nathan continued to survey the trees.

"This is a new experience for them," she whispered to Ryan.

"Sorry, Sarah. I should have suggested this sooner."

"We're not your responsibility, Ryan." She didn't want to be a burden.

"Yes, you are." His intense gaze brought back last night's dream. Blushing, she looked away. "I don't want you to feel that you have to look out for us."

Well, that didn't sit well. Ryan stopped and she bumped right into him. Turning, he cupped her elbows in his gloved hands. The boys had wandered up ahead. "But what if I want to?"

She blinked up at him. "Want to what?"

"Do a lot of things. For you. With you. If you'll let me." His eyes pleaded.

The cold air must be getting to her. Ryan probably was talking about shoveling her sidewalk, not the vivid, body melting dreams that had kept her sleepless since the movie in South Haven.

"Sarah?" He lowered his head, as if to kiss her.

*Oh, give me a sign, Jamie.*

"Mom!" Justin's voice brought them back to reality.

"Coming." She could barely push the word through her trembling lips.

Ryan scorched her with a glance. Snow fell from a nearby tree.

"Come on. Let's catch up." Taking her hand, he pulled her forward. Good thing because her legs had turned to cookie dough.

They'd come to a patch of smaller trees. "These look about right, don't you think, Nathan? Justin?" Sarah called out. The boys had wandered up ahead.

"No, not these." Nathan glanced back and saw their hands clasped. Elbowing Justin, he gave his brother a pleased smile. She wiggled her hand from Ryan's grasp, not that she wanted to.

They kept walking. Whatever the boys had in mind, these trees weren't passing muster.

"You have to shake the snow off," Ryan told the boys. "That way you have a better idea of how it will look in your house."

Sarah chuckled as the boys got busy, grabbing limbs and shaking. Most of the snow ended up on them. As she stood there enjoying the sight, a snowball hit her right in the back. Turning, she found Ryan laughing, his smile gleaming in the sun.

"You stinker. All right. You asked for it." Scooping up some snow, she packed it tight and aimed. Ryan didn't know, but she was pretty good at this. The snowball exploded against one broad shoulder.

"Game on, Sarah." Unhooking the chainsaw, Ryan reached down. Giggling, Nathan and Justin joined in the fun. Snowballs whizzed through the crisp air and some found their mark. Sarah packed hers light and lobbed them toward Nathan and Justin. But Ryan? He got the full force of her aim. The boys shrieked with laughter, cheeks rosy as they threw haphazard mounds of snow at Ryan and Sarah. The craziness lasted for a few minutes, until they were all gasping for breath.

"Snow angels," Sarah called out, not wanting the fun to end. Falling back, she worked her arms to form wings. Nathan and Justin joined her, arms and legs flailing in the snow. But Ryan only watched, as if he were taking it all in, a big smile on his face. But they'd come on a mission. "Back to work," Sarah finally said.

Holding out a hand, Ryan helped her up.

"That was the most fun I've had in a while," she admitted, brushing the snow from her green jacket.

"You need more fun."

*I need more of you.*

But of course she couldn't say that.

Ryan retrieved his chainsaw. "Guess we should get that tree."

As they moved on, Ryan fell in beside her. "Your cheeks are all red."

"I must be a mess." She jabbed at her headband.

Ryan stopped and helped her adjust it. "You look cute."

Sarah felt the crazy impulse to kiss him.

"Sarah," he said, his eyes holding the kiss she wanted imprinted on her lips.

"The boys," she whispered.

He edged away. They kept walking.

Gradually, her pulse stopped hammering in her ears. "Thanks for bringing us." Up ahead, the boys had gone back to shaking snow from the trees.

"It's fun for me too, Sarah." He smiled down at her.

Dazed, she murmured, "I'm glad."

His steps slowed. "You know what I'd like to do, right?"

Heat flushed Sarah's face. "Yes. But the boys."

"Right." He looked around. "It's so peaceful here."

Away from the bakery, she felt responsibilities fall away, like the snow dropping from the trees. "Before we came out here, it didn't feel like Christmas, know what I mean? The real Christmas. The holiday of peace and...love."

"Not even during the Holiday Walk?" Forehead furrowed, he looked puzzled.

"Don't take it personally." She gave him a poke. "Santa won't even give me a clue about what my children want for Christmas."

Ryan glanced up ahead where the boys were circling smaller trees. "Some things are sacred. Kind of like scout's honor."

She narrowed a glance at him. "You were a Boy Scout?"

"Heck no." He looked horrified.

Ah, that bad boy look was back. "Way too tame for you, right?"

"Sort of." But Ryan didn't look as if he wanted to own that. "Do you think we're getting closer?"

"Sorry." She drew away.

Grabbing her hand, he tugged her toward him. "I meant closer to the right tree."

"Maybe. Who knows what they have in mind?" Their linked hands felt way too good and she broke away. "Nathan and Justin might see us."

He nodded up ahead. "Looks like they're plenty busy. Would that be so bad, Sarah?"

"Not really. I guess." The feelings running through her were real, not from a feverish dream. Reality shook her. She drew in a frigid breath. "Did your parents bring you and Jamie here?"

His chuckle echoed in the quiet woods. "Are you kidding? My mother hated the cold so Dad had to get the tree. She gave him strict instructions. One year he even had to take a tree back and exchange it."

"No way." Now, that got her laughing. "That poor man."

Looking down at her, he smiled. "You see the good in everything. Everyone."

"That's very sweet." The urge to kiss Ryan twisted inside her, and she felt relieved when Nathan called out, "I see it! I see it, Uncle Ryan. The perfect Christmas tree."

"I can't wait." Her breath froze white on the air as she hustled to catch up. Then she skidded to a halt and shot Ryan a glance. His surprised expression mirrored her own amazement.

This had to be the most pathetic tree she'd ever seen. Just a few inches taller than the boys, the poor thing listed to one side, its thin branches reaching for the ground. "Oh, honey. Are you sure?"

"This is it," Nathan said and Justin nodded his agreement.

Sarah swallowed. "It's kind of small. Maybe we'll come back in a couple of years. Meanwhile, we can take one of the other trees home." She glanced around. They all looked better than this one.

"Make that ten years," Ryan muttered from the corner of his mouth.

But her sons didn't agree.

"The tree needs us, Mom." Nathan gently fingered the needles of a scrawny bough. "We can make this the best Christmas tree ever."

She seriously doubted it. "Might take a lot of work." Leaning to one side, the tree had maybe ten branches, if that. And they all aimed in different directions.

Nathan's lower lip came out. "If we give it a lot of love, it'll grow, like those flowers you brought home last summer."

Kate had given Sarah a flat of zinnias that had gone without water too long. Sarah nursed them back to life. "But this is a tree, sweetheart. Trees don't grow that quickly."

Nathan didn't look convinced.

"This is our Charlie Brown tree," Justin chimed in. "Like the TV show."

They seemed so certain. She hated to disappoint them. Sarah glanced over to Ryan, who lifted his shoulders. "Looks like the boys have made up their minds."

"You've gotta have hope, Mom." Something in Nathan's voice pinched Sarah's heart. Had she lost all hope after what had happened to her family? She sure hoped not. Did the size of the tree matter? After all, the Christmas tree was for the boys. And it sure wouldn't take much time to decorate. "Okay then. Let's take our tree home."

When Ryan pulled the ripcord on the saw, the boys' eyes lit up like Christmas bulbs. Sarah hadn't seen them this excited in a long time.

"At least I can drag this one to the truck without too much trouble," Ryan said above the rattle of the saw.

"Are you kidding? Even I could carry this tree." One

disapproving look from Nathan and she shut up. Before too long, the tree surrendered with a graceful swoosh.

"Are you two going to help me?" Ryan turned off the saw and hooked it back on shoulder harness. Both boys nodded, eager to get their hands on the tree.

"Good. I'll take the bottom and you two take the top." Ryan hoisted the tree and the boys fell in behind him.

The day was crystal clear as they trudged through the snow, the base of the skinny tree resting on Ryan's shoulder while Nathan and Justin tended to the top. When they reached the truck, the tree fit perfectly in the back, its slender trunk extending just a bit. Ryan tied a red flag on it. Then they took off for home.

All the way back, the boys craned their necks to see out the back window to make sure the tree hadn't fallen out of the truck.

"Don't worry," Ryan said with a chuckle. "That tree isn't going anywhere."

"Thank you," she mouthed silently to him.

His smile widened. When he reached for her hand, she linked her fingers with his. Every so often, he brushed a thumb over her hand. The ride home wasn't long enough for her.

Back at their bungalow, they took the tree through the French doors. The tree fit perfectly in the corner next to the fireplace. Watching Ryan position the tree in the large green and red stand, she knew she would remember this for a long time.

"Do you have the decorations?" Ryan asked.

"In the hallway. I brought them down from the attic."

"I would've done that for you, Sarah." She heard the frustration in his voice.

"It's not a problem, Ryan. I'm used to taking care of myself." She watched him fume. "What?" The boys were in the hall and she heard them pop the top off one of the bins.

"I enjoy doing things for you," Ryan said quietly.

She felt something unlock inside. "And I like it too. So I guess I'll just shut up."

"Here's the angel, Mom." Nathan rushed into the room. "For the top of the tree."

The glittery angel with its outstretched wings would dwarf this poor tree. "It's getting late. We'll save that for tomorrow, okay?"

Night had fallen so quickly. "Maybe we should decorate the tree tomorrow night. Grandma Lila can help us." Sarah knew her mother would find that fun.

"Oh, Mom." Their faces drooped.

They both looked tired. "School tomorrow. Ryan and I have to get up early and work."

Standing in the doorway, Ryan hesitated.

"You'll come help us decorate, won't you?" she asked, remembering what he'd just said about helping her.

"I'd like that," he said with a slow grin.

"I'll make chili."

"You don't have to feed me."

"Maybe I want to."

They stood there, tossing words at each other like colorful ribbons that bind a gift together.

But it was getting late. "Boys, give your Uncle Ryan a hug and then up to bed."

How it warmed her heart to see Ryan scoop the boys up one by one to give them a bear hug. He really loved them, and they adored him.

"See you tomorrow?" He turned to her before he left.

She followed him to the back door. "You're allowed to sleep in late tomorrow."

His eyes twinkled. "I don't even know what that means."

"You'll probably have those ovens roaring by the time I get there." The hug caught her by surprise. Ryan smelled of warm sheepskin and the pine tree, and his arms felt so good around her.

"Is...is this okay, Sarah?" he asked drawing back.

"Yes, it sure is." But it was getting late. Hands on his chest she pushed away. "Now you be careful on those roads."

Behind her the boys giggled. Without turning around she said, "You'd better be upstairs before I count to ten. One...two..." The old stairs creaked as they scurried up to bed.

"Well, good night." For a second he looked undecided. Then he opened his arms and she fell into them. The kiss brushed her lips but ignited her entire body.

Giving her a final soft hug, Ryan released her. "I better go."

"Night." Feeling dazed as she stood in the doorway, she watched Ryan get into his truck and start the engine. She saw the quick turn of his head and a final wave before she closed the door. The glass panes felt cool against her forehead when she rested her spinning head against them. Sarah sure hoped she knew what she was doing. Her lips burning, she slowly went upstairs to tuck the boys in. They were talking. Hand on the door, she waited before pushing it open.

"Do you think it's working, Nathan?" Justin asked.

"Yep. Just like we planned," her oldest answered with smug satisfaction.

Whatever were they talking about?

She poked her head in the door. "Did you brush your teeth?"

"Yes, Mom." Looking guilty as heck, they snuggled down under the warm blue quilts Lila had given them last Christmas.

"Did you have fun?" Sarah perched on the bottom of Nathan's twin bed.

"We like being with Uncle Ryan," Nathan said. "Don't we, Justin?"

Her youngest nodded, eyes swerving to his big brother, as if they shared a secret.

"What's going on here?" Her mom radar went up.

"Mom, do you like Uncle Ryan?" Nathan asked slowly.

"Of course, I do. I've always liked your uncle." Well, that was only partially true.

"That's good." Justin settled back.

"Do you think he'd show me how to use that saw?" Nathan made a sound like a chainsaw, one that would chill any mother's heart.

"Maybe. But not until you're older." She gave them one more kiss and then left the door open a crack. The night light was on in the hallway.

Walking back downstairs, she locked up. Their pathetic little

Christmas tree sure didn't look like much. Some of the branches hugged the trunk, straight up. Yep, this was a sorry sight. "Little tree, what are we going to do with you?" The house smelled heavenly, though. Nuking some water in the microwave, she stirred in some sugar, just as Lila had taught her. Then she added some cold water so the mixture was warm but not hot and added it to the tree stand.

"Drink this up, little tree. It will help you keep your needles until after Christmas." Then she fixed herself some cinnamon peach tea and settled onto the sofa. Her life was so busy that she rarely had these moments.

Without any lights or ornaments, the tree tugged at her heart.

"You and me, kiddo," she told the tree. "We need a redo."

Sitting there, she felt the Christmas season fill her heart. If she could string together these happy moments, then maybe she could rebuild her life. After all, wasn't that what Christmas was all about? Hope and love.

She felt the weird sensation of teetering on the brink of something. The feelings she had for Ryan grew deeper every time they were together. Running her fingers gently over her lips, she closed her eyes and relived that kiss. Yep, she sure liked it. Pushing up from the sofa, she turned out the lights and went to bed.

Later, as she lay with the covers up to her chin, she had her usual conversation with Jamie.

"The boys had such a good time today, picking out a tree. You should have seen them. But the tree's pretty pathetic. You wouldn't believe it. The boys had fun, though. They love Ryan. And I..." But she carefully placed the picture back on the nightstand.

*Oh, Jamie. Please send me a sign.*

~.~

As he carried a tray of fresh bread to the front the following morning, he overheard Sarah talking to her mother. And he stopped. They'd mentioned his name. So he rested the tray of cookies he'd been bringing out and listened. Sure, this was eavesdropping. He didn't care.

Sarah had just said something like, "I'm so glad you're moving on."

"Aren't you jumping to conclusions?" Lila said. "After all, Stuart and I just met."

"But he really likes you, Mom. I can tell. And you should move on, shouldn't you? I mean, it's time."

The sound he heard sounded like a sigh. Or maybe it was just the wind whistling through the leaky door in the back. Ryan edged closer.

"Oh, Sarah, how can you measure what the right time is? It's about the man, not any set amount of time."

Silence. Ryan was afraid to move.

"Is it that simple, Mom?" Sarah finally asked.

Ryan stepped back. Clearly, this was a personal moment.

"It is, sweetheart. When the man is right, it's that simple."

*All right!* Ryan brought a knee up and pumped a fist. His knee banged the tray and lemon bars went flying everywhere.

"What is going on back here?" Sarah peeked around the swinging door. Her face fell when she saw the mess. "Oh dear."

"I-I just tripped," he stammered, scrambling to pick up the bars. "Maybe these can be saved."

"Oh, I don't think so." She helped him clean up.

"I'll start a new batch. But first I need more coffee." He escaped to the front, wanting to hug Lila as he passed.

"So did you choose the perfect Christmas tree?" she asked while he filled his mug with coffee.

Ryan shook his head. "I don't know how perfect it is. But they like it."

Sarah joined them, wiping her hands on her apron. After yesterday, he could hardly look at her without wanting more. But this morning she couldn't meet his eyes. Was she mad about the lemon bars?

"Your mom just asked me about the tree," he said. "Is it perfect?"

"Perfectly awful," Sarah said, pursing the lips he really wanted to kiss again. "But it's the tree the boys wanted."

"Really? I'm all ears." Lila's mom was wearing a Christmas sweater with reindeer on each side in sparkles. Before, Ryan never noticed what she wore. Now she was brighter. More cheerful. Must be the librarian and he was happy for her.

Walking over, Sarah filled her mug with coffee. "Remember the Charlie Brown Christmas show?"

"Of course. We watched that every year, remember? Charlie Brown picked out a scrawny tree that needed all the tender love and care he could give. I loved that show and so did you."

"Well that's what we have in our living room." And Sarah didn't sound very happy about it. "I can't picture our decorations on that tree."

He didn't want her worrying about that. "I'll help you decorate. Look. It's snowing again." As Ryan walked to the window, he felt Lila's eyes on him and turned.

Sarah's mother tilted her head. "Something is different about you, Ryan, and I can't figure out what it is."

"Just the same old me." Time to head back to the workroom.

But before he could escape, a light went on in Lila's eyes. "You're walking differently. Did you have surgery or something?"

Sarah studied him. "That's silly, Mom. Of course not."

Time to come clean. Ryan kicked out a boot. "Just had my boots adjusted a little."

"How did I miss this?" Sarah's hands went to her pink cheeks. "I've been with you every day and I didn't notice."

"It's no big deal, Sarah." The last thing he wanted was her studying his limp.

The bell over the door jingled. Cold air gusted in along with an older man with a cardboard carrier holding three steaming cups. They sure smelled good. "Good morning."

"Hello, Stuart." Beaming at the guy, Lila introduced them.

So this was the librarian.

The man nodded. "I'd shake your hand but mine are full."

"Let me take those." Putting down his mug, Ryan grabbed the carrier and set it on the counter.

"You've all been so good to me, sharing your delicious cookies," Stuart said. "I thought I might share what I learned from my family about coffee."

"Well, aren't you the one?" Lila gave Stuart a look that made Sarah blush.

Ryan was enjoying the whole thing.

Stuart started handing out cups, and Ryan set his mug aside. "As I told you at the library, Sarah, my family is in the coffee business. And I've learned quite a bit."

"He has all kinds of fancy machines in his kitchen," her mother said.

The remark seemed to catch Sarah by surprise, and she exchanged a look with Ryan. Then she took a sip from the cup in her hand. "Caramel?"

Stuart nodded. "Like it?"

"Love it. What do you have, Mom?"

"Gingerbread," her mother said with a pleased smile. "My favorite."

"I know." Stuart gave Sarah's mother another adoring look. But he tore his eyes away to focus on Ryan. "How do you like the peppermint?"

"Delicious." Ryan wasn't a fan of peppermint but he saw where the older man was going.

Stuart eyed their coffee pot in the corner. "Sarah and I have been talking about the coffee part of this business," Ryan said.

"Yes, we have," Sarah admitted, feeling like they'd come to a turning point. "Daddy did start this as a coffee shop, Mom."

Her mother toyed with the top of the cup. "Oh, I know." She eyed the large machine behind the counter with trepidation.

"This machine is a relic," Stuart told Lila softly. "A newer model would be easier for you to operate."

"Would it?" Mom said, defeat in her voice. "We're so busy."

"You want to be busy, Lila. At some point, one of the coffee companies is going to open a shop in Gull Harbor or out on Red Arrow Highway," Stuart pointed out. "Those outfits usually put in some baked goods too. Not bread, but definitely pastries."

Her mother gave a soft gasp. Sarah's face paled. She set the warm coffee on the counter. "That would be a disaster."

Ryan hated to see her like this. "But that doesn't have to happen," he said. Her frown eased a bit.

Stuart was nodding. "Ryan is right. I'll be happy to kick around some ideas with you to make sure that doesn't happen."

"Maybe after the new year," she said, running a hand over her forehead.

Would Stuart even be here next year? Ryan would be back at Branson Motors full time. He'd miss this place. And Sarah. They should move on this now. "I know you're busy right now, Sarah, getting ready for Christmas," Ryan said slowly. "Would it be all right if I kick some ideas around with Stuart?"

"Oh, I don't know." She didn't look convinced. "I hate to take up your time."

"January and February would be a good time to makes changes," Stuart suggested. "After the holiday rush."

Lila was looking at her daughter. Sarah was the decision maker now.

Ryan wasn't about to let this go. "It wouldn't take long to come up with some ideas. You and your mom could look them over. You wouldn't have to be involved."

Her eyes cloudy, Sarah turned to him. "Are you sure you have time?"

"I'll make time. It's just a coffee machine, Sarah." With relief, he watched her frown fade.

"Well then, I guess we'll move ahead." Picking up her cup, she took a gulp.

"Good." Relief washed through him, and Stuart looked pleased.

"To Christmas and new beginnings," Sarah said, holding up the coffee.

Ryan liked the sound of that. He didn't want Sarah or her mother to be put into a bad spot. Jamie wouldn't have wanted that. Suddenly Ryan saw that his promise to his brother held more than just watching over Jamie's family. Was he ready for the job? That might be up to Sarah.

After Stuart left, Ryan got back to work. He was zesting a lemon for more lemon bars when he felt a soft touch on his shoulder.

"I'm so sorry," Sarah whispered.

He turned. "What about?"

She pointed to his boot. "I never noticed. It's just not what I..."

"What?" Settling against the counter, he pulled her closer, one eye on the swinging door.

"I guess it's not what's important to me, Ryan," she whispered. "Although I know it is to you."

"Let's forget about it." And he tucked a curl into her hair net.

"This net is such a sexy look."

"Are you teasing me?" She pouted in the cutest way. If Sarah had a little girl, this is what she'd look like.

Ryan hoped he'd see that one day.

# Chapter 11

How could chili burn in a slow cooker? Sarah was a hot mess. Ryan would be here any minute and the smell of burnt food filled the house. Opening a can of diced tomatoes and more tomato paste, she dumped them into the pot and ran upstairs to get ready. When the front door bell rang, she had just finished a shower and was pulling on a pair of jeans that were way too tight and her red V-neck sweater.

"Nathan, would you please get the door!" she called downstairs.

"No problem, Mom." She heard the door open. "Come on in, Uncle Ryan."

Was that her oldest son speaking, so polite and welcoming? A dash of red lipstick and she was ready.

As she came downstairs, Ryan looked up. Their eyes locked and she smiled. "Hey, how were the roads?"

"Not bad." He stripped off his gloves and the big sheepskin coat. Instead of toeing off his snowy boots, Ryan rubbed them carefully on the throw rug near the door. This was all about the boot and his leg. She got that now.

Rubbing his hands together, Ryan sniffed the air. "Something sure smells..." His nose wrinkled.

"Burned?" She draped his jacket over the rocking chair and dropped his gloves near the air vent to dry. "Hope you enjoy burned chili."

"As long as I don't have to make it, fine with me." He grinned. "I've always liked your chili, Sarah. Some things never change."

By that time Justin had traded the TV for a hug from Uncle Ryan.

"Come and see the tree," Nathan said, tugging on his uncle's hand.

"I helped you get it. We put it in the stand together, remember?" Still, he let himself be pulled into the living room.

"Some of the crooked branches won't come down." Justin said, very matter-of-fact.

"Down?" Ryan looked alarmed. Then he saw the tree. The poor little thing. Its bare branches reached out, as if it needed help. "Bigger trees might have kept this poor little guy in the shade. See where the branches are all crooked. Have you got your decorations ready?"

"The boxes are right here," Sarah said coming up behind them. "They're a little dusty."

"So I see." Turning, he smiled at her. Then his fingers brushed her curly hair.

"What? Do I look terrible?" Her hands went to her hair.

"No, you look cute. Thanks for inviting me today." Ryan caught her hand and gave it a squeeze that went straight to her heart. As they stood there talking, Nathan exchanged a look with Justin. Those boys. Always up to something.

Ryan carried the green tubs from the hallway and stacked them in front of the tree. She had the strings of lights set out on the coffee table. "I told you I'd do that, Sarah."

"I know you did. But you weren't around. Besides, I'm used to..."

"Doing things yourself?" He looked miffed.

"Don't take it the wrong way, Ryan." She touched the elbow of his navy sweater. "My mother always tells me I have to let other people do things for me."

"Your mother's a wise woman." His eyes swept her face, stopping at her lips and mercy, she felt them plump.

"I'm used to doing everything myself." She could hardly squeeze the words through her swollen lips. The lips that so badly wanted to kiss him.

"I know. But people will help you."

"People like you?" she said.

"Exactly. Just tell me what you need."

*I need you.*

What were they doing? Nathan and Justin stood close by, watching them the way they'd watched that toy train circle the track in the toy shop. She clapped her hands. "Boys, let's get going. Lights first?" She turned to Ryan.

"Sure." But when Ryan lifted them from the coffee table, the boys didn't look thrilled. "I thought we were using the big lights this time, " Nathan said, eyeing the miniature lights with disgust.

"You mean the big, colored lights?" Sarah had decided they were too old-fashioned. She was surprised that he remembered.

Both boys nodded. "Okay, I'll go get them."

"Let me help." Ryan looked to the boys for help. "Guys, can you hold down the fort?"

"Sure. Of course." They exchanged another look.

"Maybe pick out smaller ornaments so the branches don't sag from the weight," Sarah told them from the stairway.

The boys got to work and Ryan followed her upstairs. In the narrow hallway she pulled at the chain that lowered a staircase and flicked on the light.

Upstairs, they both ducked under the rafters. The attic was freezing and she shivered. "Just point," Ryan said.

She motioned to the three green tubs stacked in a corner. "They're marked."

"Got it." But when he went to move around her, Sarah lost her balance. The space was so cramped.

"You okay?" Grabbing her arms, Ryan steadied her.

"No." She could only shake her head. "No, I'm not. And I don't know what's wrong."

One arm came around her waist and he cradled her head in his other hand. "Don't let things get you down this Christmas."

"I'm trying." His words soothed her. Still, they had a job to do. "I'm glad you came today."

The attic was freezing but his kiss warmed her. Her eyes fluttered shut. Just one kiss and then he pulled back.

"Don't stop. Not yet." Sarah didn't open her eyes. His kiss was comfort and she needed more.

"Oh, Sarah."

Ryan's second kiss touched her heart, his lips sweet and gentle. Sarah tightened her arms around his neck. "I've been thinking about this since the other night," she murmured, rubbing her nose on his.

He pulled back and grinned. "Good. So have I."

"But is this right, Ryan?" Uncertainty prickled in the back of her mind.

"It's right in every way. But you have to feel that way too, Sarah."

She laid a finger on his lips. Felt the bristle of his stubble on her skin. "I think I'm worrying about nothing,"

His low laugh awakened every nerve in her body. "And I think you're right."

"Mom?" Nathan's voice rose from the bottom of the ladder.

"Coming," she called down.

"Where are those lights?" Ryan peered at the tubs.

"Lights." She pointed to the one with a label she recognized. He dragged it to the top of the stairs and together they carefully negotiated the ladder.

Downstairs, the boys had hung a couple of smaller ornaments on the tree. But it would take a lot to make these sparse boughs look festive. At least the needles were still on the tree. She'd checked that morning and they were soft and pliant in her fingers. Could have been her imagination but the branches seemed a deeper green than before. Ryan opened the box and took out the old-fashioned lights. The boys' eyes widened. Big and multicolored, they'd dwarf the tiny tree. Ryan began stringing the lights.

"Should we eat first and then decorate?" she asked.

"I want to decorate now." It was unusual for Justin to speak up first. "Our tree looks lonely."

"Oh, sweetheart." But what could Sarah say? The tree was puny—a real rescue tree. No matter how they turned the poor thing, it had no good side.

Ryan shrugged. "It's up to your mom."

Nathan and Justin were so eager to start. She remembered that feeling. "When we feel hungry, we'll eat. How's that?" Everyone nodded and Ryan continued working on the lights. But her mind and heart were still back in the attic, and her body was definitely still in his arms, where she'd felt safe and warm. After dropping one ornament, that promptly shattered on the floor, she let the boys do the decorating. Her hands were shaking. And it was more than a kiss that made her lightheaded. Being here with Ryan and the boys felt so right. Sarah felt as if she'd walked into a room she'd never been in before but it felt familiar.

"I thought your mother might be here." Ryan looked around.

Laughing, Sarah scooped a cranberry garland from one of the tubs. "She had other plans."

"Grandma has a boyfriend," Nathan said solemnly.

Picking up a box of ornaments, Ryan smiled. "Do you like Stuart?"

"He's nice," Justin said.

"For an old person," Nathan added. Ryan and Sarah both laughed.

Ignoring their advice about size, Nathan hooked one of the

largest green ornaments on a bottom limb. The poor branch quivered and sagged to the floor.

"Oh, no!" Nathan looked horrified. "I broke the tree."

"I think we have to be careful with this little guy," Ryan said, handing Nathan one of the angels made from colored yarn and glitter. As soon as Nathan made the switch, the lower branch sprang back to life. Decorating this tree was like giving someone artificial respiration.

"Will the tree grow?" Justin asked very seriously as they decorated.

Ryan stepped back. "We'll just wait and see." When he clicked on the lights, the tree blazed to life. Sarah was amazed by all the color. The old bulbs brought back fond memories and hid the tree's shortcomings.

"It's beautiful." Nathan stood back to admire it.

"Wow." Justin's eyes couldn't get any bigger.

Ryan slipped an arm around Sarah's waist and whispered words for her ears alone. The room grew very quiet. Looking up, Sarah saw both boys watching them intently. "Guess I'll check the chili." She leapt toward the kitchen.

Ornament by ornament, the little tree took shape. The boys kept the decorations smaller and lighter, which helped. Still, in spots Sarah feared the branch would break. Since their traditional Christmas angel was way too big for the top, they settled on a simple straw star.

"It's perfect." This tree sure wasn't what Sarah had in mind. But if the boys thought it was beautiful, she was satisfied.

"It looks just like the Charlie Brown Christmas tree," Justin said with satisfaction after they'd added some tinsel to fill in the bare spaces. Nathan nodded.

Sarah glanced over at Ryan, who seemed to agree. "Is that your stomach I hear growling?"

"Maybe." He patted his flat stomach with one hand, a lazy gesture that rocketed her from the sofa.

"Just give me a minute."

"Want me to start a fire?" Ryan gave her a look that warmed her clear to her toes.

Maybe he already had. "Sure. The wood's outside the back door." This would be the first fire of the season. Between work and the boys, Sarah never had time to fuss with the fireplace. Before she knew it, the boys were helping their uncle. Together they carried in pieces of firewood and crunched up newspaper to get the fire started. Working in the kitchen, she soon heard the crackle of the fire in the living room.

Coming to the doorway, she smiled. "This is beautiful." The fire gave the room a warm glow that made her wonder why she didn't do this more often.

Crouched in front of the fire, Ryan turned. "Pretty cool, right?"

"Spectacular." Besides the fire, the only light in the room came from the tree, reflecting on the ornaments. Caught in the spell of the homey scene, she set the dining room table instead of the kitchen so they could see the tree. As they chowed down on the chili and sour dough bread, the boys couldn't stop looking at the tree and the fire. Their excitement reminded her that the beauty of

Christmas lay in small things. The lights. The old ornaments. The fire. Having Ryan here.

Which reminded her. "You'll come for Christmas, won't you, Ryan?"

"Yeah, you'll be here, right?" Nathan said.

"All day Christmas," Justin added.

Sprinkling more cheese on his chili, Ryan threw her a shy grin. "Thought you'd never ask."

"Well, of course we want you here."

As they sat there eating and planning, Sarah couldn't help but think about Jamie. This wasn't how she'd pictured this Christmas a year ago. But the encouragement of her mother and Lindsay came back to her. What good would it be for her and the boys to stay stuck in the past? No way would she allow them to dwell on their loss. Jamie wouldn't have wanted that. Nathan and Justin should have lives full of love, friends and family.

And so should she.

By the time they finished dinner, it was time for the boys to go to bed. "Both of you, say goodnight to Uncle Ryan and then get upstairs. I'll come up and tuck you in."

For a change they didn't argue. Maybe they were tired out from working on the tree. Nathan gave his uncle a ferocious hug. Sarah didn't know what had gotten into him. "Easy, Nathan." But Ryan patted his back, as if he understood the insecurities inside that determined little boy.

Not only did Justin hug Ryan, he also gave him a peck on the cheek. Kissing the top of Justin's head, Ryan turned away. But not before she saw tears glimmering in his eyes.

He was a tough guy who cared.

The boys scampered upstairs. Not long after she heard the water turn off, she went up to kiss them goodnight. They were already fast asleep.

Ryan helped her clear the table. "All that fresh air knocked them out," Sarah said, as she set the dishwasher. The liner of the slow cooker had been soaking. Now she dumped the water out and grabber her scrubber brush.

"Here, let me." And with that, she was muscled out of the way. Not that she minded.

"You'll spoil me," she murmured, folding the dish towels.

"I hope you'll let me."

"Let you?" Teasingly, she nicked his chin with a towel.

Ryan set down the scrubber. "You know what I mean."

"Why don't you show me?" Was this really her talking?

"Come here." And with that, he pulled Sarah to him. Because she wasn't proud of her waist right now, she squirmed a little.

"What?" Leaning back, he peered down.

"You're holding my love handles." She had to be totally honest with him.

"Sweet Sarah," he groaned, tightening his hold and nibbling her neck. "Isn't this what love handles are for?"

"Not really. My ten ugly pounds are in your hands."

"You don't have any ugly pounds. You're perfect."

"And you're kind," she murmured, while his lips drove her crazy. "My neck is ticklish. But my mouth isn't."

With a low chuckle that she felt deep in her stomach, Ryan sealed his lips over hers. The sweetness heated quickly—like the brown sugar syrup she used in her pecan rolls when she turned the heat up high. Leaving the kitchen, they cuddled in front of the fire on her old green plaid sofa. The flames threw shadows that flickered over the magical scene. Sarah wanted to savor the special moment.

This evening felt right. Even their little Christmas tree seemed to be winking at them.

Saying goodnight was so hard.

"I want to take this slow," he said at the door.

"Me too. But it won't be easy."

Ryan had her cocooned inside his jacket. Playing with his rumpled shirt, she wanted to stay there, cared for and cozy. A cold wind rattled the door.

Gently backing away, he snapped up his jacket. "Guess I should go."

"Yep. Guess so." One more quick kiss and he pushed the door open.

"See you, Sarah."

"Good night." How she hated to close the door, but her teeth were chattering. Outside his truck roared to life. Pushing back the curtain, she watched the truck until he put his blinker on and turned.

The room felt empty without him, except for the tree. Sarah collapsed in the rocker. "I sure hope I know what I'm doing," she told the little tree. "How are you holding up?" Falling to her knees, she felt the water pan. Dry and she trotted out to the kitchen to fill a pitcher. "You've got to make it through the holidays," she said, filling the pan.

With all the lights off, the tree glowed, a beacon of hope.

"Good night, little tree." She clicked the lights off and dragged herself upstairs.

Somehow she got her pajamas on. After brushing her teeth, she huddled in her bed, Jamie's picture on her knees. "See, here's the thing, Jamie," she told him. "I really care about Ryan. And I think you'd like the fine man he's turned out to be. No more reckless stunts. He's good with the boys."

Kissing her finger, she pressed it to the glass like always. Setting the picture on her bedside table, she sighed. "If you could give me a sign, Jamie. Let me know that what I'm doing, how I'm feeling about Ryan, well....just let me know it's okay. Somehow."

## Chapter 12

"Mommy, Mommy!" The boys' excited voices woke Sarah up the next morning. Bleary-eyed, she stumbled down the stairs.

"What is it?" In the early morning darkness, the lights glowed in the living room. "Did you turn the tree on?"

Nathan's chin came out. "I'm a big boy."

Sighing, she slipped onto the sofa, wishing it still held Ryan's warmth. "I know you are, sweetheart. But what's the problem? What time is it anyway?"

"The tree." Sitting cross legged in front of their tiny tree, Justin looked up as if he were seeing Santa himself in those boughs.

The boughs. "My word. What happened?" Who had slipped into the house in the middle of a winter's night to swap out their pathetic excuse for a Christmas tree for this beauty?

The luscious smell of pine hung in the air, as heavy and thick as the branches on their Christmas tree. Melting onto the sofa, Sarah could only stare. The configuration was the same, but the tree seemed fuller. She drew closer. "The crooked branches had sagged into the bare spaces. The tree still wasn't perfect, but it was theirs.

"Santa must have come and helped our little tree," Nathan said with the outrageous belief of a five year-old. "There are more needles on it."

"Or maybe a Christmas angel." There could only be one explanation. She pulled her legs up under her.

*Thank you, my love.*

Some things are beyond human logic. Sarah let her suspicions rest with that explanation. Blessed by love, the tree carried a message that transcended time and space. The message had reached her and Sarah cradled it in her heart.

Their heat was set to click on at six in the morning, and the cold floor told her it wasn't that time yet. Too early to get up. Shaking out the green afghan, she beckoned to Nathan and Justin. "Come here, boys. Let's cuddle."

"But I want to look at the tree," Justin said, his fingers skimming over the boughs.

"And that's exactly what we're going to do."

The boys piled onto the sofa and together they shared their warmth. Savoring the tree, now resplendent in its glory, Sarah knew in spirit there were four of them.

Ryan was whistling "I'm Dreaming of a White Christmas" when he came down the steps early the next morning. That was Lila's holiday favorite and he caught her humming it all the time. After the evening with Sarah and the kids, he felt totally content. Burned chili and all, decorating the tree took him back to his childhood and the experiences shared with his brother. Somehow Jamie always made things right. That's how the evening had felt...right.

A cool blue moon shone through the high windows of the garage, glancing off the Harleys and cars in the darkened shop. Branson Motors had been his world for a long time. But maybe that was changing. He'd had a call on his phone from Stuart. They were going to meet about the new business plan for The Full Cup.

The light was on in the office.

"Who's making all that noise?" Stanley called out.

Smiling to himself, Ryan stepped around the tools and vehicles and made his way back.

"Sounds like you're the one yelling, old man." Ryan leaned against the doorframe. "Is that your breakfast?"

"Want some instant oatmeal?" Stanley kept a hot plate back here. He held up a mug that said Cranky Old Geezer.

"I'll take the coffee but hold off on the oatmeal." Stepping over, he poured himself a cup of steaming coffee and sat down. He'd gotten up earlier today. As happy as he was, he couldn't sleep.

Peering at him over the lip of his mug, Stanley took a sip. "So what's with the whistling?"

"Just feeling pretty good right now." Slouching in the hardback chair, he smiled.

Stanley's eyes twinkled. "So the widow woman's working out, is she?"

Ryan wasn't about to share any details. "Let's just say, we're happy where we are right now."

"Yeah, well something put that smile on your face. You look happier than a red bulb on a Christmas tree."

"By the way, thanks for letting us use your woods. You've got some beautiful acreage there."

"Did you get a tree? I haven't been out there much since the snow started."

The tree. Ryan didn't know what to say. "We saw a lot of awesome trees. But Nathan and Justin chose the most pathetic tree you've ever seen."

Stanley sat up like he'd been hit with a cattle prod. "In my woods?"

"Sorry, but yes. Relax. That's why they liked it. The boys said it was their Charlie Brown Christmas tree. Fits real nice in the corner of Sarah's living room. I was kind of relieved. Some of your trees are so big, I could never have wrangled one into Sarah's small bungalow."

"Glad it worked out. So everything's fine?" Stanley paused, obviously curious.

"Guess so." Ryan tossed back the last mouthful of coffee and stood up. "See you later. I have to go make gingerbread men."

"Do tell. You're getting all proper on us now." Raising a pinkie, Stanley took a small sip of his coffee."

As Ryan was striding through the garage, Stanley called out, "I could use some of those gingerbread cookies with my coffee!"

Ryan chuckled until he hit the frigid air outside. Man, it was cold. His ears stung as he pulled himself up into the cab. Sitting there waiting for the truck to warm up, he could not stop thinking about Sarah. But she hadn't been the only one on his mind all night as he tossed and turned in bed. No, Jamie had been there too, running through his head with his straight-shooting, confident ways.

The one message Ryan heard was "Go for it"—his brother's favorite phrase. In his dreams, Jamie was smiling when he said it.

Ryan threw the truck into drive. *Okay, I will, big brother. I sure will.*

~.~

By the time Sarah got to The Full Cup, Ryan had filled the racks with breads, brownies, lemon bars and even some gingerbread men. "What is this?" She shrugged off her coat. "What time did you get here?"

"Early," he said with the cutest duck of his head. Who knew a guy could look masculine with a frosting bag in his hand.

"Wow, I'm impressed." Grinning, she tied on an apron. "You almost look as if you know what you're doing."

Sliding a tray of gingerbread men onto the counter, he gave her a dark look. "Oh, I do. I know exactly what I'm doing."

She grabbed a second bag and another load of cookies. "Let's time ourselves. Winner gets her wish."

Coming closer, Ryan snagged her by the waist. His kiss was coffee-delicious. "Maybe the winner will get *his* wish."

So he wanted a challenge? "Game on." It wasn't easy to pull herself from his arms, but she sprinted to the other side of the counter and positioned her tray, one eye on the clock.

"Go!" They both ducked their heads.

Sarah worked faster than she ever had before. She tried not to let her excitement put too much pressure on the piping bag. Halfway through her tray, she looked up. Hunched over, Ryan nipped his lower lip as he worked. That one glance nearly broke her rhythm.

When she took the tray from the cooling rack, she hadn't really paid much attention to the cookies on it. Wielding the bag of frosting with ease, she sped through the gingerbread men, Santa Claus and Christmas tree cookies. But the entwined R and S caught her by surprise. Sarah's throat closed and her eyes blurred.

She couldn't rush through this. Hands shaking a bit, she took her time, piping a pretty scroll along the lettering.

Ryan startled her when he shouted out, "Done!"

"Oh, you are just so pleased with yourself," she muttered, still working on her last cookie.

Peering over her shoulder, he murmured, "So, what do you think of my work?"

"That you can be pretty devious." Zipping around, she shot a string of frosting that landed right below his left eye. She got him pretty good.

Hooking her with one hand, he laid down his bag and laced his hands behind her back. "I think you owe me."

Reaching up, she swept the frosting from his cheek. "Aw, you're so sweet, Ryan."

"Never thought I'd ever hear that. Are you mocking me?" His eyes turned deliciously dangerous.

"No, never." Giggling, she couldn't offer any resistance as he pushed her toward the door to the shop. "What are you doing? It's almost time to open."

"Later. Right now I have other ideas."

She looked up. The mistletoe. "Perfect."

The conversation was cut off by a Christmas kiss she'd remember forever. Tunneling her fingers through Ryan's thick hair, she felt the rasp of his beard and something else. Her cheek felt sticky. "You're getting frosting all over me."

"Turn around is fair play." What a stinker. Ryan turned his cheek just a bit until both their faces were a gooey mess.

"Stop. Stop." But her voice was choked by giggles.

"What is going on?"

Sarah and Ryan turned. Frosting obscuring one eye, she had trouble seeing her mother, standing there with hands on her hips. But Mom was laughing.

After Ryan left for Branson Motors, Sarah grabbed her blue binder, just to make sure they were covering the bases. She flipped open the cover and stared. The recipes were divided by plastic tabs, each section alphabetized. When she opened to Cookies, her recipes were arranged neatly. Each scrawled note, card or piece of torn newspaper safely encased in a plastic slip sheet. This had to be Ryan's work and her heart turned over.

Amazed, she lugged the binder out to her mother.

"Will you look at this?" Sarah set the binder down and opened it.

"Oh, my." Her mother whisked through the pages. "Ryan did this?"

"I guess so. Do you believe it?"

Turning, her mother gave her a slow smile. "I'd say this man's a keeper."

# Epilogue

## *Six months later*

A saw whined and hammers pounded from the workshop Ryan had built in the yard. The sweet smell of sawdust and early summer hung in the air. Would the man ever stop working? Sarah was thrilled that Ryan was enlarging the deck. But not today. "Mom and Stuart will be here soon!" she called out.

The saw stopped. Ryan appeared in the doorway of the shed. No man wore a T-shirt and jeans like her husband, safety glasses shoved back on his head. "What's that, babe?"

The grass tickled her bare feet as she strolled toward him. Sarah was still getting used to Ryan working in what used to be *her* backyard.

*My husband. Our backyard.*

She liked it.

Looping an arm around his neck, she cuddled closer. "Time to clean up," she whispered. "Mom and Stuart are coming over, remember?"

After a leisurely Sunday afternoon kiss, Ryan pulled away. "Got it. Gee, you smell good." His chest expanded when he inhaled.

"I'm all shampooed and showered." She tapped that broad chest with a finger. "Your turn."

The rat-tat-tat of hammers had stopped inside the shed. Nathan and Justin came to the door. "They're at it again." Nathan rolled his eyes. "Disgusting."

Smiling, Justin followed his brother outside. "I know. Kissing all the time."

"Are we disgusting?" Sarah murmured.

Ryan smiled down. "Never."

"Last one to the swing is a rotten egg!" Nathan dropped a pint-size hammer and ran. Justin did the same.

Ryan held up a hand and the boys lurched to a stop. "Hey, first put those hammers back where you got them, okay?"

"Yessir." Scooping up the hammer, Nathan dashed back into the shed, his brother right behind him. Then it was off to the new swing set Ryan had put up this spring.

Since their wedding on Valentine's Day, Ryan had fixed every loose hinge, stubborn doorknob and leaky window in her house. Now working at The Full Cup, he strategized with Stuart about the new espresso line. The cold winter helped make the flavored coffees an instant success. How relieved Sarah had felt, sending off that final overdue tax installment.

But most important, he'd been spending a lot of time with the boys in the evenings and weekends. Stanley and Ryder Branson had understood when Ryan told them that family came first. He wouldn't be able to put in any hours at Branson Motors. But he sometimes stopped at the garage for coffee, and Sarah had invited Phoebe and Ryder over for supper, along with Stanley. Ryder's dad was a real hoot.

While Ryan was showering, Mom and Stuart pulled into the driveway. Hollering at the top of their lungs, Nathan and Justin streaked toward the car. You'd think the two newly-weds had been gone all month, instead of two weeks. How cute they were together as they got out of the car, starry-eyed after their honeymoon in Tuscany.

"I think you two picked up a tan over there." Sarah linked arms with her mother, walking with them into the back yard. "You both look great."

"Don't know about the tan but I did pick up ten pounds," Stuart laughed. "How's business?"

"Good, but I'm glad you're back in town."

They settled at the picnic table. After Sarah brought out lemonade, her mother told her all about Italy.

Good news. Now everything seemed to be good news.

But she was waiting for Ryan before sharing theirs.

Looking around the yard, Sarah thought back to the time when she'd wondered how she could handle all this. How could she raise the boys and run The Full Cup alone? Now she had the full support of a growing family. The library had hired a new director and Stuart had started working part time at the coffee shop. He fit right in and was especially helpful with the sleek espresso machine he'd given Mom for Christmas.

The screen door whapped shut. "Welcome back," Ryan called out. His hair wet from the shower, he smelled like soap when he slid in next to her. "Did you give them the news?"

Her mother perked up. "What news?"

Sarah had been hugging their secret to her heart. "We're having a baby."

Her mother lit up like that dear little tree they'd had last Christmas. "Oh, sweetheart. I'm so happy." She sniffled.

Handing Mom his handkerchief, Stuart looked stunned. "Will that make me a grandfather?"

"You already are," Nathan told him.

"Yeah, you're our grandpa," Justin added, his tone suggesting Stuart should have known this.

"Now, don't you go lifting any of those heavy trays at work," her mother warned her.

"Don't worry. I won't." While they talked about the due date, Sarah felt Ryan's eyes on her. She squeezed his hand, so grateful for everything that had come their way since Christmas.

"Any idea about, you know, boy or girl?" Her mother waited.

"Ye-es," Sarah said slowly. "We had the ultrasound last week."

The air quivered with anticipation. "It's a girl." Cripes, tears stung her eyes. Lately, she was so darn emotional.

"A little girl," Mom said with wonder.

"Yeah." Nathan rested his chin on one hand "Mom says we have to be really good to her. Big brothers and all that."

That tadpole feeling shimmered deep in Sarah's tummy, as if this little girl were introducing herself. "Sometimes I can't believe it."

"Any idea about names?" Mom asked.

"All decided." Sarah and Ryan smiled at each other with quiet certainty. "We're going to call her Jamie."

## THE END

## Other Books by Barbara Lohr

**Enjoy more sweet Gull Harbor stories with the
Man from Yesterday series**

Coming Home to You
Always on His Mind
In His Eyes
Late Bloomer
Still Now Over You
Every Breath You Take

**Take a trip to Sweetwater Creek with the
From Best Friends to Forever series.**
Marry Me, Jackson
Steal My Heart, Trevor
Christmas with Dr. Darling
(coming in November 2019)

**Enjoy romance in Chicago, Savannah or Italy with the**

**Windy City Romance series**

Finding Southern Comfort
Her Favorite Mistake
Her Favorite Honeymoon
Her Favorite Hot Doc
The Christmas Baby Bundle
Rescuing the Reluctant Groom
The Southern Comfort Christmas

*Note: All books in each series stand alone and can be read
separately or in sequence.*

## About the Author

Barbara Lohr writes sweet contemporary romance, with all its heart tugging, funny moments. The *Man from Yesterday* series takes place in Gull Harbor, a charming beach town where the second time around truly is better than ever. Barbara's *Best Friends to Forever* series takes readers to Sweetwater Creek, where life moves a little slower and love develops with a slow, rich sweetness. Although set in Oak Park, a suburb of Chicago, the *Windy City Romance* stories take readers on fabulous journeys of the heart to Savannah, Tuscany or Guatemala.

Barbara lives in the South of the US with her husband and their cat, who insists that he was Heathcliff in another life. In addition to travel, her interests include golf, kayaking and cooking. She makes a mean popover. Friend her on Facebook or connect on Twitter. She loves to hear from readers.

www.BarbaraLohrAuthor.com

www.facebook.com/Barbaralohrauthor

www.twitter.com/BarbaraJLohr

# A Word from the Author

Many thanks to Romance Writers of America, a group whose members are generous with their knowledge base. The loops and forums of writers who address writing and publishing issues are invaluable to me.

To my readers, thank you! Your appreciation and support warm my heart. Keep responding to my newsletters and be sure to enter my giveaways. I sure appreciate your interest and hope to continue to write books that take you on "journeys of the heart," as one of you mentioned.

For my daughters Kelly and Shannon, keep those reading lamps on over your beds. For us, reading has always been a tie that binds. My grandchildren Bo and Gianna bring me such joy and of course pop up in Mama B's novels. To my husband Ted, words aren't adequate to thank you for your love and support, especially when my computer crashes and you provide tech support. May we have many more wonderful years together with trips to Leopold's for ice cream.

Made in the USA
Columbia, SC
12 November 2019